BUDDHA

ブッダ

8: *Jetavana*

THE JOURNEY

NEPAL

ROHTAK◎

◎MEERUT

◎MORADABAD

DELHI◎

◎BAREILLY

◎ALIGARH

◎SHAHJAHANPUR

CAPITAL OF KOSALA

JETAVA

MATHURA◎

SAVATTHI

AGRA◎

UTTAR PRADESH

KOSALA

◎JAIPUR

SAKETA

◎ LUCKNOW

FAIZABAD

CHAMBAL R.

◎KANPUR

◎GWALIOR

YAMUNA R.

THE GANGES

PRAYAG

ALLAHABAD◎

• KOSAMBI

JETAVANA

KAPILAVASTU

KUSINAGARA

DEER PARK

LUMBINI | ANCIENT PLACE NAMES ——— MAJOR ROUTES • PLACES VISITED BY THE BUDDHA

TIBET

▲ MT. DHAULAGIRI

THE HIMALAYAS

MT. EVEREST

KATHMANDU

BHUTAN

YEARS AS PRINCE

KAPILAVASTU

PLACE OF BIRTH

LUMBINI

RAMAGRAMA

KUSINAGARA

NIRVANA

GORAKHPUR

MITHILA

PLAINS OF HINDUSTAN

SECOND COUNCIL

BHASHARA R.

DARBHANGA

VAISHALI

THE GANGES RIVER

FIRST SERMON

SARNATH

PANTA

PATALIGRAMA

DEER PARK

VARANASI

MAGADHA

BHAGALPUR

CHAMPA

NALANDA

GAYA

RAJGRIHA

BIHAR

BODH GAYA

EAGLE PEAK

BANGLADESH

LOTUS SUTRA

1ST COUNCIL, CAPITAL OF MAGADHA

SON R.

ENLIGHT-ENMENT

THE GANGES

INDIA

ASANSOL

RANCHI

BARDDHAMAN

WEST BENGAL

JAMSHEDPUR

CALCUTTA

KHARAGPUR

EAGLE PEAK

BAY OF BENGAL

HarperCollins*Publishers*
77–85 Fulham Palace Road,
Hammersmith, London W6 8JB

www.harpercollins.co.uk

Published by HarperCollins*Publishers* 2006

ISBN-13 978-0-00-722458-6

The artwork of the original has been produced as a mirror image
in order to conform with English language.
This work of fiction contains characters and episodes
that are not part of the historical record.

Printed and bound in Great Britain by
Clays Limited, St Ives PLC

Mixed Sources
Product group from well-managed
forests and other controlled sources
www.fsc.org   Cert no. SW-COC-001806
© 1996 Forest Stewardship Council
FSC

FSC is a non-profit international organisation established to promote the
responsible management of the world's forests. Products carrying the FSC
label are independently certified to assure consumers that they come
from forests that are managed to meet the social, economic and
ecological needs of present and future generations.

Find out more about HarperCollins and the environment at
www.harpercollins.co.uk/green

PART SIX (CONTINUED)

PART SEVEN

PART SIX (CONTINUED)

CHAPTER EIGHT

DEVADATTA'S PLOT

PRINCE AJATASATTU HAD BEEN IMPRISONED IN THE NORTHERN TOWER FOR FOUR YEARS. HE HAD JUST TURNED 17.

HOWEVER, YEARS OF TEDIOUS IMPRISONMENT WITH NOTHING TO DO BUT STEW IN ANGER HAD CHANGED HIM SO MUCH THAT HE LOOKED FAR OLDER THAN HIS YEARS.

ACCORDING TO THIS, BUDDHA PREACHED TO PRINCE CRYSTAL AND GOT HIM TO TAKE HIS ARMY OUT OF KAPILAVASTU.

THAT'S CORRECT, PRINCE.

DAMN THAT SLICK-TALKING BUDDHA! AS IF DUPING FATHER WASN'T ENOUGH, NOW HE'S GOT PRINCE CRYSTAL ON A LEASH.

WONDER WHAT HE SAID TO GET THAT COCKY PRINCE TO ROLL OVER, PLAY DEAD AND SEND HIS TROOPS HOME.

CHEEP CHEEP

OH, HELLO AGAIN.

MEET MY NEW FRIENDS.

THEY COME ALL THE TIME NOW TO EAT THE LEFTOVER RICE FROM MY MEAL.

THEY NEVER DARE TO SIT ON MY HAND, THOUGH.

11

I HAVE TO STAY IN JAIL AT LEAST 5 MORE YEARS, RIGHT? THAT'S THE PUNISHMENT THAT FATHER ORDERED!

INDEED, HIS MAJESTY GAVE SUCH AN ORDER 4 YEARS AGO.

BUT IF THE KING BECAME INCAPABLE OF RULING HIS COUNTRY, HE WOULD HAVE NO CHOICE BUT TO HAND THE THRONE TO THE PRINCE, CORRECT?

INCAPABLE? WHAT DO YOU MEAN?

A FEW DAYS AGO, THE KING'S HEALTH TOOK A TURN FOR THE WORSE.

IS HE SICK?!

NO, HE IS NOT SICK AT ALL.

HE HAS FITS, SPASMS. HIS CHEST ACHES, AND HE WRITHES ABOUT LIKE ONE POSSESSED.

THE DOCTORS TRIED TO FIND A CAUSE, BUT ALL THEY DISCOVER IS THAT HE WAS SOMEHOW... POISONED.

BUT IF HE'S NOT SICK, THEN WHY HASN'T HE GOTTEN BETTER?

BECAUSE FOR 4 YEARS, A CERTAIN POTION HAS BEEN SECRETLY MIXED INTO HIS DRINK.

THE DRUG IS NOT AT ALL POISONOUS

BUT IT IS POWERFUL, AND THEREFORE HIGHLY ADDICTIVE.

THEREFORE, WHEN ONE STOPS TAKING THE DRUG, THE WITHDRAWAL SYMPTOMS CAN BE QUITE PAINFUL.

SO WHAT'S GOING TO HAPPEN?

AS THINGS STAND, HE IS INCAPABLE OF RULING THIS COUNTRY.

THE PRIME MINISTER AND MANY HIGH-RANKING OFFICIALS THINK THAT GIVING YOU THE THRONE IS THE ONLY WAY TO KEEP THE GOVERNMENT FROM FALLING APART.

WHAT THE HELL HAVE YOU DONE? HOW DARE YOU!

YOU'VE PLANNED THIS FOR 4 YEARS?

FOR YOUR SAKE, PRINCE, DID I DO THIS. I WOULD DO ANYTHING FOR YOU.

I WILL ALWAYS BE YOUR BEST ALLY, PRINCE.

SO WHAT'S THE REST OF YOUR PLAN? WHAT DO YOU WANT IN RETURN FOR MY FREEDOM?

I NEED YOUR SUPPORT IN ORDER TO TAKE CONTROL OF VENUVANA! PLEASE HELP ME!

BUDDHA'S GONE. HE WON'T BE BACK FOR A WHILE. VENUVANA HAS NO LEADER!

PLEASE, SIR...

WHY DO YOU WANT TO RULE VENUVANA?

WITH YOUR BLESSING, I COULD CREATE A POWERFUL RELIGIOUS SECT.

I ASKED BUDDHA TO MAKE ME HIS SUCCESSOR 3 YEARS AGO, BUT HE REFUSED. HE'S STUBBORN. SO STUBBORN THAT HE REFUSES TO SEE GREATNESS IN OTHERS.

DEVADATTA... YOU'RE MY OLDEST, MOST FAITHFUL FRIEND.

IF YOU GET ME OUT OF THIS PLACE, I WOULD DO EVERYTHING IN MY POWER TO HELP YOU.

THANK YOU, DEAR PRINCE.

I WILL BRING GOOD TIDINGS SOON.

I'M LEAVING.

VENUVANA WILL BE MINE!

15

VENUVANA

BAD NEWS!!

WHAT'S YOUR PROBLEM?

IT'S NOT MY PROBLEM!

THERE'S TROUBLE BREWING IN THE CAPITAL!

THE KING HAS LOST HIS MIND!

KING BIMBISARA HAS GONE INSANE, YOU SAY?

HE GETS TERRIBLE FITS. HE FROTHS AT THE MOUTH AND HIS EYES BUG OUT OF HIS HEAD!

THAT'S AWFUL!

DR. ZIWAKA EXAMINED HIM. HE THINKS SOMEONE POISONED HIM!

MORE NEWS! PRINCE AJATASATTU HAS BEEN RELEASED FROM PRISON!

AJATASATTU? THEY LOCKED HIM UP AFTER HE SHOT BUDDHA.

HE'S OUTTA JAIL? SOMETHING'S FISHY HERE...

WHAT'S GOING TO HAPPEN TO THE DEMO-CRATS?

LET'S NOT GO THERE.

SARIPUTTA, MOGGALLANA, HAVE YOU HEARD THE RUMOR?

YES, WE CAUGHT WIND OF IT WHILE WE WERE OUT BEGGING FOR FOOD.

THIS IS SERIOUS. A POWER STRUGGLE FOR THE THRONE WON'T BLOW OVER EASILY.

BUT WE CAN'T ALLOW OURSELVES TO GET CAUGHT UP IN THIS AFFAIR.

WELL, WE MIGHT GET DRAGGED INTO IT WHETHER WE LIKE IT OR NOT...

BUT PLEASE STAY CALM. WE CAN'T AFFORD TO KICK UP A FUSS WITH BUDDHA GONE.

WHO GOES THERE?

KING AJATASATTU WROTE THIS WITH HIS OWN HAND. READ IT WELL.

HMM...

I PROCLAIM TO ALL SAMANNA IN VENUVANA: AS OF TODAY, X-DAY OF Y-MONTH IN Z-YEAR, DEVADATTA IS RECOGNIZED AS YOUR LEADER. IF YOU DO NOT OBEY HIS COMMAND, YOU MUST FORSAKE THE SECT AND EVACUATE THE PREMISES IMMEDIATELY.

HMMM...

WHAT

WHAT

WHAT

ABSURD!!

I REFUSE!!

BUDDHA IS THE REASON WE CAME TO THIS PLACE!

I WON'T TAKE ORDERS FROM THE LIKES OF YOU!

BUT KING AJATASATTU HAS ORDERED YOU TO OBEY.

21

WHAT A SPOILED BRAT.

THIS IS AN OUTRAGE!!

DO YOU REALLY THINK YOU HAVE THE STUFF TO LEAD THIS GROUP, DEVADATTA?

OF COURSE! I'VE GOT WHAT IT TAKES TO TURN THIS INTO A FINE RELIGIOUS GROUP!

WE ALREADY NUMBER A THOUSAND! I'VE GOT BIG PLANS FOR DEVELOPMENT! IF BUDDHA'S TEACHINGS COULD BE SHARED WITH THE REST OF THE WORLD, WE'D CONVERT HUNDREDS OF MILLIONS OF PEOPLE! JUST HEAR ME OUT!

I DON'T THINK BUDDHA WOULD APPROVE.

SHOULDN'T WE WAIT UNTIL HE RETURNS?

THAT PROCLAMATION IS EFFECTIVE AS OF TODAY! YOU RISK ARREST IF YOU PUT IT OFF FOR EVEN A DAY!

22

WELL, IF YOU'RE GONNA LEAD

THEN I'M GONNA LEAVE.

HEY, COOL IT, NADI...

DEVADATTA, WE HAVE TO FOLLOW THIS PROCLAMATION TO THE LETTER?

OF COURSE. KING'S ORDERS.

WELL, THEN, IF WE MUST DO EXACTLY AS WRITTEN...

THIS SAYS "SAMANNA OF VENUVANA" MUST FOLLOW YOU, BUT NOT ALL SAMANNA.

SO NOT EVERYONE NEED ACCEPT YOU AS THEIR LEADER. IN OTHER WORDS, IF JUST A PART OF THE GROUP CHOSE YOU, EVERYONE ELSE CAN FOLLOW WHOMEVER THEY PLEASE.

WHA-?!

DON'T NITPICK!!

ATTA BOY, SARIPU-TTA!

LET'S GATHER EVERYONE TOGETHER AND FIND OUT HOW MANY MONKS WISH TO FOLLOW YOU.

...

I'M JUST FOLLOWING ORDERS, EXACTLY AS WAS WRITTEN IN THE PROCLAMATION.

24

25

27

...

IF YOU WISH TO FOLLOW ME

POINT YOUR FINGER HIGH UP TO THE HEAVENS!

YEAH!

SPIELBERG!

DAMN...

BARELY A QUARTER RAISED THEIR HANDS.

SARIPUTTA SURE DID A GOOD JOB OF PULLING THE WOOL OVER THEIR EYES.

WELL THEN... ALL THOSE WHO RAISED YOUR HANDS, GATHER YOUR THINGS AND MEET ME TOMORROW MORNING BY THE FOREST EDGE.

29

ELEPHANT'S HEAD MOUNTAIN WAS WHERE BUDDHA PREACHED TO THE KASSAPA SECT ABOUT FIRE. DEVADATTA AND HIS FACTION OF THE DIVIDED MONKS CHOSE THAT SPECIAL MOUNTAIN AS THEIR POST FOR THE TIME BEING.

WAIT HERE. I'LL GO TO MAGADHA AND REQUEST A MEETING WITH KING AJATASATTU. HE'LL DO ANYTHING I ASK OF HIM.

TAKE THE OLD KING AND LOCK HIM UP IN THE NORTH TOWER. I WANT A GUARD THERE FULL TIME. HE IS NOT TO BE ALLOWED OUT UNDER ANY CIRCUMSTANCES.

THE KING IS GRAVELY ILL, MY LORD...

SUCH TREATMENT SMACKS OF FILIAL IMPIETY.

KEEP COMPLAINING AND I'LL LOCK YOU IN THERE TOO, MINISTER.

I AM KING. I MAKE THE DECISIONS.

YOU MUST OBEY MY ORDERS.

I SHALL OBEY...

HIS MAJESTY HAS ORDERED THE OLD KING TO BE LOCKED INTO THE NORTH TOWER.

WHAT ?!

I FORBID YOU TO DO ANY SUCH THING!

MINISTER, BIMBISARA IS IN CRITICAL CONDITION!

KING'S ORDERS, DOC. DON'T WHINE.

BUT THAT'S RUTHLESS! IF YOU PUT HIM IN THAT HELL-HOLE, HE'LL DIE!

DR. ZIWAKA, YOU COULD STILL ATTEND TO HIM IN THE TOWER.

I KNOW HOW YOU FEEL BUT OUR HEADS WILL ROLL IF WE DON'T FOLLOW ORDERS.

BETTER TO JUST GO WITH THE FLOW. JUST FOR A LITTLE WHILE.

MAJESTY!

HAVE YOU NO HEART...?

I BEG YOU, LET YOUR FATHER OUT OF THAT TOWER, RIGHT AWAY!

THIS IS NOTHING MORE THAN COLD-BLOODED REVENGE!

I CAN HARDLY BELIEVE THAT MY OWN FLESH AND BLOOD COULD BECOME SUCH A MONSTER!

MAJESTY, YOUR MOTHER IS ON HER KNEES, BEGGING YOU TO STOP THIS SPITEFUL DEED!

FATHER IS THE ONE WHOSE HEART WAS POISONED BY A MONSTER. HE NEEDS TO BE KEPT OUT OF THE WAY UNTIL HE'S BETTER. WHAT'S WRONG WITH THAT?

NO, IT WASN'T A MONSTER. IT WAS DEVADATTA! FOR YEARS HE'S BEEN MIXING SOME STRANGE POTION INTO HIS DRINK!

34

HUMPH!

AND JUST WHAT MAKES YOU THINK THAT?

DEVADATTA HIMSELF TOLD ME HE DID IT!

THAT MAN IS AS WILY AS A SCORPION, A SNAKE! ARREST HIM AND ASK HIM ABOUT IT YOURSELF!

MOTHER!

YOU ARE NO LONGER QUEEN HERE.

TAKE HER TO THE WOMEN'S QUARTERS AND DON'T LET HER OUT.

I WILL NOT TOLERATE YOU MEDDLING IN MY AFFAIRS!

MAJESTY!

UHN...

 UHHH...

I—IT... IT HURTS!
H—HURTS...
SO MUCH...

W—WHY...
WHY
AM I...

UNH...
UUHHH
!

 AARGH!
UHHN!

 OH, IT
HURTS!!
S—SOME-
BODY...
HELP ME!
AAAH!

 FIRST THE
PRINCE WAS
LOCKED IN
HERE. NOW
THE OLD KING
HAS TAKEN
HIS PLACE.

IS THIS
WHAT
THEY CALL
KARMA?
UNBELIEV-
ABLE.

IS THAT YOU, DEVADATTA?

300 LOYAL MONKS HAVE DEFECTED FROM VENUVANA. THEY'RE CAMPED AT ELEPHANT'S HEAD MOUNTAIN.

OH?

ONLY 300 MONKS?

LESS THAN I HAD HOPED FOR. BUT FEAR NOT, I'LL CONVINCE EVERY LAST ONE OF THEM TO LEAVE BUDDHA.

YOU'RE NOWHERE NEAR AS POPULAR AS I THOUGHT YOU WERE.

WELL, THAT'S ONLY BECAUSE THEY HAVEN'T SEEN MY TRUE COLORS YET.

BUT WITH YOUR ENDORSEMENT, EVERY SAMANNA IN INDIA WILL BOW DOWN TO MY LEADERSHIP.

CLERK!

GO TELL THE MINISTER OF FINANCE

THAT I ORDER 10 JARS OF GOLD PIECES TO BE GIVEN TO DEVADATTA.

THANK YOU VERY MUCH FOR YOUR SUPPORT. I AM IN YOUR DEBT.

TAKE THAT MONEY AND BUILD THE COUNTRY'S BIGGEST MONASTERY. THAT WAY ALL OF INDIA WILL KNOW THAT YOUR SECT IS THE GREATEST.

YOU'RE TOO KIND, BUT THE RULES OF MONKHOOD DON'T ALLOW SUCH INDULGENCES. SAMANNA MUST SLEEP OUTDOORS, WEAR RAGS AND FORAGE FOR WILD NUTS AND SEEDS.

AN EXTRAVAGANT TEMPLE WOULD GIVE THE WRONG MESSAGE.

THAT'S A SHAME.

SO YOU'RE SAYING YOU DON'T WANT ALL THAT MONEY?

NO, SIR. I WAS PLANNING ON DONATING IT TO CHARITY. IN YOUR NAME, OF COURSE.

I SEE. YOU'RE SO GOOD TO ME.

ELEPHANT'S
HEAD
MOUNTAIN

40

YOU DON'T REALLY BELIEVE ANY GOOD WILL COME OF BETRAYING BUDDHA LIKE THIS, DO YOU?

WHEN WILL YOU STOP NAGGING ME ABOUT THIS?

DEVADATTA'S A SMOOTH TALKER...

AND HE'S A GENIUS. BUT NO MATTER HOW YOU LOOK AT IT, YOU'RE STILL A TRAITOR TO BUDDHA.

I GET IT ALREADY!

BUT DEVADATTA IS MY FRIEND. I OWE HIM. HE'S THE REASON I'VE GOT A GOOD REP IN MAGADHA. I CAN'T TURN ON HIM.

BUT YOU'D TURN AGAINST BUDDHA? DON'T YOU OWE HIM, TOO?

DEVADATTA'S GONE TO THE CASTLE. NOW'S OUR CHANCE. LET'S GO BACK TO VENUVANA.

QUITCHER NAGGIN'. GO BACK TO BED.

41

ALL RIGHT, I GIVE UP.

I'LL JUST RUN TO KAPILAVASTU AND TALK TO THE MAN HIMSELF.

WHAT ?!

YEAH, NOW I'VE GOT IT!

I'LL GO GET BUDDHA'S PERMISSION! IF HE WON'T LEMME DO IT, THEN I'LL JUST GO HOME TO VENUVANA.

Y-YOU'D GO THAT FAR JUST TO ASK PERMISSION ?

DON'T! IT'LL TAKE WEEKS, MAYBE A WHOLE MONTH TO GET THERE!

NAW, I'LL GET THERE IN A JIFFY. I'LL JUST STEAL A HORSE OR SOMETHING.

WHAT DID I TELL YA? TEZUKA KNOWS HOW TO TAKE CARE OF HIS CHARACTERS.

I'LL BE BACK IN A HEART-BEAT...

BE GOOD TO YER MUM, KIDS.

TATTA, DON'T GO YET...

WHAT? WHY?

I DON'T KNOW, I'VE GOT A FUNNY FEELING...

...LIKE I MIGHT NOT SEE YOU EVER AGAIN.

WORRY WORT! I'LL BE BACK REAL SOON!

43

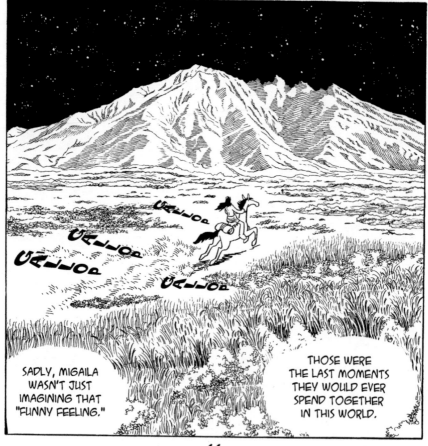

SADLY, MIGAILA WASN'T JUST IMAGINING THAT "FUNNY FEELING."

THOSE WERE THE LAST MOMENTS THEY WOULD EVER SPEND TOGETHER IN THIS WORLD.

DO YOU REALLY THINK YOU CAN GET THOSE MONKS TO COME BACK TO VENUVANA?

YEAH, PROBA-BLY.

I GUESS YOU'VE GOT A PLAN IN MIND, MR. BRAIN.

I DO. NOT THE MOST HONEST PLAN, BUT IF A LITTLE TRICKERY BRINGS EVERYONE BACK TOGETHER IT'S OK, RIGHT?

YOU'RE GOING TO TRICK THEM?

WE SHOULD GET THERE BY DAWN, I THINK.

THE MOUNTAINS ARE USUALLY FOGGY AROUND DAYBREAK. I'M GOING TO USE THAT TO MY ADVANTAGE.

HEY, MIGAILA. WAKE UP.

IT'S ME, SARIPUTTA!

OH HI, SARIPUTTA! HAVE YOU DECIDED TO JOIN DEVADATTA'S MONKS?

HA! QUITE THE OPPOSITE. I'M BRINGING EVERYONE BACK TO VENUVANA.

WHERE'S DEVADATTA?

HE'S GONE TO THE CASTLE TO SPEAK WITH THE KING.

WHO'S THERE? THAT VOICE SOUNDS FAMILIAR.

IT'S SARIPUTTA!

MOGGAL-LANA'S HERE, TOO!

LOOK AT ALL THIS FOG!

EVERYONE, PLEASE LISTEN UP!

LAST NIGHT, I WAS VISITED BY A HEAVENLY MESSENGER. I COULD FEEL HIM BECKONING ME TO LISTEN!

I CAME HERE ON HIS COMMAND. HE SAID I MUST BRING EVERYONE BACK HOME TO VENUVANA!

SORRY TO DISAPPOINT YOU, SARIPUTTA, BUT WE DON'T EVEN WANT TO PHONE HOME.

THAT SAME HOLY MESSENGER HAS BEEN SO GRACIOUS AS TO ACCOMPANY ME HERE.

REALLY? THERE'S AN ANGEL HERE?

WHERE IS HE?

HE'S STANDING RIGHT BEHIND ME! LOOK, LOOK!

WOW!

IT'S TRUE!!

HEAVENS! LOOK, YOU CAN SEE HIS HALO!

THE HOLY MESSENGER SAYS THAT DEVADATTA'S SCHEME IS SHEER BLASPHEMY.

PLEASE, COME BACK TO VENUVANA.

I CAN'T BEAR THE THOUGHT OF EVERYONE BEING PUNISHED FOR DEVADATTA'S MISCHIEF.

49

BUT WE CAN'T ASSUME THAT NONE OF THOSE MONKS KNEW ABOUT THAT ILLUSION. SURELY A FEW MONKS CAUGHT ON TO SARIPUTTA'S TRICK. SOME SAY THAT OUT OF RESPECT FOR SARIPUTTA, THEY KEPT QUIET AND FOLLOWED ALONG.

OTHERS SAY THAT EVERYONE WAS SECRETLY HOPING FOR AN EXCUSE TO GO BACK TO VENUVANA. NOT ONLY WAS ELEPHANT'S HEAD VERY COLD AT NIGHT, BUT MANY FEARED TROUBLE WAS BREWING AMONG THE MONKS.

TATTA! MIGAILA! THE KING HAS PLEDGED MONEY FOR US!

HEY, TATTA!

WHERE IS EVERYONE ?!

IS ANYONE HERE ?!

CHAPTER NINE

NARADATTA

AROUND THE SAME TIME, BUDDHA, ANANDA AND VISAKHA WERE MAKING THEIR WAY TO KOSALA. THE NEWLY DISCIPLED RAHULA, BHADDIYA, ANURUDHA AND KIMBILA JOINED THEM ON THEIR JOURNEY.

AH, THIS IS GREAT! I COULDN'T BE HAPPIER!

YOU'RE A JOLLY FELLOW.

HA HA HA... WELL, YOU SEE, I'VE NEVER BEEN ABLE TO HAVE THIS MUCH FUN BEFORE.

I THOUGHT I'D BE A SLAVE FOREVER. I NEVER EXPECTED ANYTHING BUT PAIN AND HUMILIATION UNTIL MY DYING DAY.

BUT NOW I'M WITH BUDDHA! I'M FREE TO GO ABOUT AS I PLEASE! THIS IS HEAVEN ON EARTH!

BUDDHA, DO YOU KNOW ABOUT THAT HERMIT MONK WHO LIVES IN THE WOODS BY THE BORDER? HE'S BEEN LIVING THE LIFE OF AN ASCETIC SINCE YOU WERE STILL IN DIAPERS. HIS DEDICATION TO ASCETICISM IS LEGENDARY.

WHAT IS HIS NAME?

THE LOCALS CALL HIM NARADATTA, BUT I THINK HIS REAL NAME IS FART-A-LOT-A.

IF YOU DON'T MIND MAKING A LITTLE SIDE TRIP, I CAN LEAD YOU TO HIS CAVE.

I THINK I'VE HEARD ABOUT THAT MONK! HE HASN'T SPOKEN A WORD OF SENSE FOR MANY YEARS NOW.

AND HE CRAWLS AROUND ON ALL FOURS LIKE AN ANIMAL.

SO DO PEOPLE MISTAKE HIM FOR A HIMALAYAN BEAR OR SOMETHING?

THERE'S TALK OF AN ABOMINABLE SNOWMAN, TOO.

LET'S GO FIND HIM.

BUT IT'S TOTALLY OUT OF THE WAY.

PERHAPS, BUT SOMETHING TELLS ME IT'LL BE WORTHWHILE TO MEET HIM.

WELL, ISN'T THIS FUN. A DAY-TRIP THROUGH A DESOLATE, BARREN, CRAGGY RAVINE.

HEY, LOOK AT THIS!

THESE ARE HUMAN FOOTPRINTS!

AND THOSE MUST BE HAND-PRINTS.

ONLY SOMEONE WALKING ON ALL FOURS COULD LEAVE MARKS LIKE THESE.

LET'S KEEP HEADING FOR THE OTHER SIDE OF THE RAVINE.

59

UHN...
NUH...
G-GUH...

I WAS TOLD THAT YOUR NAME IS NARADATTA. IS THAT TRUE?

URG...
UNH...

?

YOU'RE TREM-BLING.

YOU'RE BURNING UP! WHAT A FEVER!

YOU'RE SO HOT THAT YOU'RE SHIVERING.

I ONLY WISH I HAD GOTTEN HERE SOONER.

60

HOO... OOH. GUH. UGH... GRRRR...

?

GUH... GOH. OHHH...

WHAT'S THE MATTER WITH YOU?

WHY WON'T YOU LET ME GIVE YOU THE MEDICINE YOU NEED?

CAN'T YOU TAKE MEDICINE?

I SEE. YOU REFUSE TO TAKE MEDICINE OR TO SEEK ANY TREATMENT. YOU'RE SAYING THAT YOU JUST WANT TO LIE THERE AND WAIT FOR DEATH?

HM?

A SPIDER SHRIVELED UP AND DIED, RIGHT IN ITS OWN WEB.

SO? DOES IT HAVE A SPECIAL MEANING?

WHAT DO YOU WANT ME TO UNDERSTAND? AH, NOW I SEE WHAT YOU'RE TRYING TO SAY...

THIS SPIDER DIED A NATURAL DEATH.

RATHER THAN FEND OFF DEATH BY TAKING MEDICINE OR SEEKING HELP, YOU WANT YOUR LIFE TO END WHEN IT'S SUPPOSED TO END, ACCORDING TO NATURE.

DID THIS MAN FORESEE HIS OWN DEATH?

I WAS A FOOL. I FAILED TO SEE YOUR WAY OF THINKING.

63

NOW I UNDERSTAND.

I WON'T DISTURB YOU ANY MORE.

WOULD YOU MIND IF I JUST SIT HERE QUIETLY AND WATCH OVER YOU?

WHERE IS THIS MAN FROM? WHAT DROVE HIM TO THESE EXTREMES? IF HE COULD SPEAK, I'M SURE HE'D HAVE A FANTASTIC STORY TO TELL.

HE'S LIVED A SOLITARY, BEAST-LIKE LIFE FOR DECADES...

HE CAN NEITHER SEE NOR SPEAK... WHAT A FRIGHTFULLY PAINFUL LIFE HE MUST HAVE LIVED.

NO, PERHAPS NOT. MAYBE AS HE GREW OLDER HE FORGOT HIS PAIN...

FORGOT WHAT IT IS TO BE HUMAN, AND LEARNED TO LIVE A PURE, CHASTE LIFE OUT HERE IN THE WILDERNESS.

DON'T WORRY. I'M FINE.

DO YOU WANT US TO JOIN YOU?

I FOUND NARADATTA IN THERE.

NO, NO NEED. I'D RATHER BE ALONE WITH HIM.

I'LL STAY THE NIGHT IN THIS CAVE.

YOU SHOULD GET SOME REST UNDER THAT BOULDER. DON'T WORRY ABOUT ME.

66

IN THE WEE HOURS OF THE MORNING, AS BUDDHA DOZED LIGHTLY, A MIRACLE OCCURRED TO NARADATTA.

A... ASITA...

A... A-ASITA!

MASTER ASITA...

HE'S SPEAKING... HE'S ABLE TO TALK AGAIN!

MASTER ASITA... H-HAVE YOU FINALLY FOR-FORGIVEN ME?

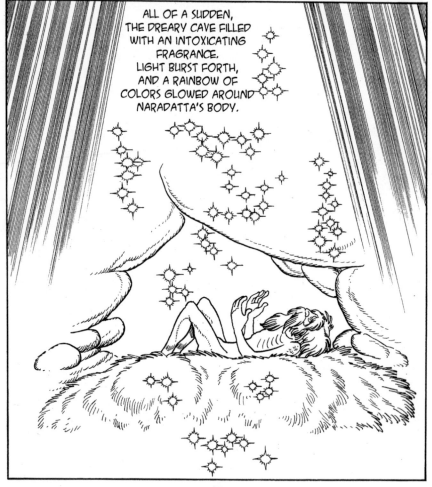

ALL OF A SUDDEN, THE DREARY CAVE FILLED WITH AN INTOXICATING FRAGRANCE. LIGHT BURST FORTH, AND A RAINBOW OF COLORS GLOWED AROUND NARADATTA'S BODY.

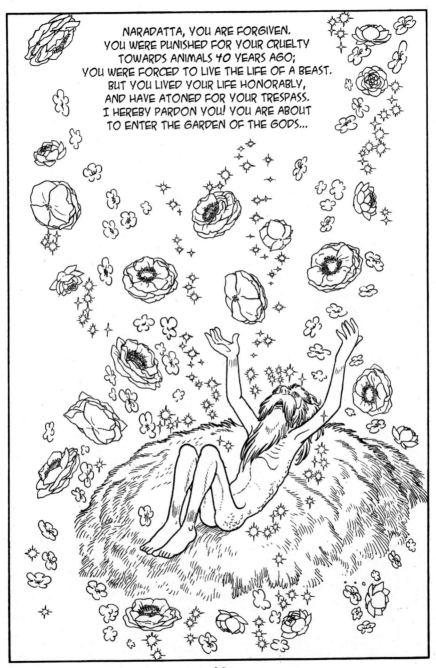

NARADATTA, YOU ARE FORGIVEN.
YOU WERE PUNISHED FOR YOUR CRUELTY
TOWARDS ANIMALS 40 YEARS AGO;
YOU WERE FORCED TO LIVE THE LIFE OF A BEAST.
BUT YOU LIVED YOUR LIFE HONORABLY,
AND HAVE ATONED FOR YOUR TRESPASS.
I HEREBY PARDON YOU! YOU ARE ABOUT
TO ENTER THE GARDEN OF THE GODS...

71

HEY LOOK, BUDDHA'S BACK!

BUDDHA! WHAT HAPPENED?

NARADATTA PASSED AWAY A LITTLE WHILE AGO.

WHAT?

SHOULD WE BRING OUT HIS REMAINS?

NO, JUST LET HIM REST WHERE HE IS. LEAVE HIS BODY FOR NATURE TO TEND TO.

WHAT KIND OF PERSON WAS HE?

A FINE MAN, FINER THAN I COULD EVER HOPE TO BE.

HE WAS CLOSER TO GOD THAN ANYONE I HAVE EVER MET IN MY LIFE.

I CAN'T IMAGINE ANYONE GREATER THAN YOU, BUDDHA.

BUT I HAVEN'T RENOUNCED THE LIFE OF HUMANKIND AND LIVED LIKE AN ANIMAL FOR 40 YEARS.

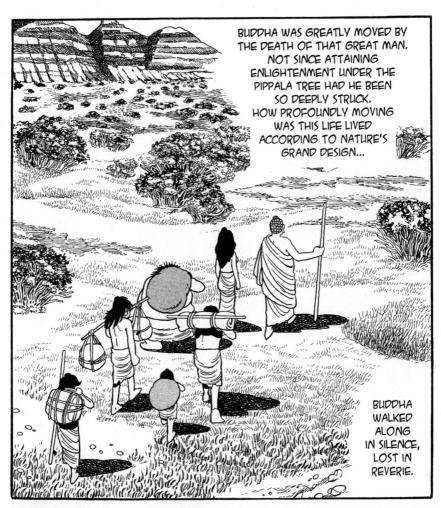

BUDDHA WAS GREATLY MOVED BY THE DEATH OF THAT GREAT MAN. NOT SINCE ATTAINING ENLIGHTENMENT UNDER THE PIPPALA TREE HAD HE BEEN SO DEEPLY STRUCK. HOW PROFOUNDLY MOVING WAS THIS LIFE LIVED ACCORDING TO NATURE'S GRAND DESIGN...

BUDDHA WALKED ALONG IN SILENCE, LOST IN REVERIE.

HE MUSED ABOUT HIS OWN DEATH. HE REALIZED THAT WHEN THE TIME CAME, HE WANTED TO GIVE OVER TO NATURE AND DIE JUST AS NARADATTA HAD.

FROM THAT
DAY ON,
BUDDHA
BROODED
OFTEN ABOUT
THE WAY
HIS OWN LIFE
WOULD END.

CHAPTER TEN

JETAVANA

SAVATTHI, KOSALA

P-PRINCE JETA...

WHAT'S A MILLIONAIRE LIKE YOU DOING HERE, SUDATTA?

I JUST WANTED TO TAKE A STROLL THROUGH THIS LOVELY PARK...

THIS IS MY PARK. YOU CAN'T JUST LOITER ABOUT AS YOU PLEASE. YOU'RE A COMMONER!

AND WHY ARE YOU ALONE? WHERE ARE YOUR SERVANTS?

WELL, YOU SEE, PRINCE...

I WAS HOPING YOU'D SELL THIS PARK TO ME.

I'VE BEEN WAITING HERE ALL MORNING JUST TO SPEAK WITH YOU.

YOU CAME TO ASK THIS FAVOR YOURSELF?

WHAT DO YOU WANT IT FOR?

WELL, ERM...

I WANT TO BUILD A MONK ESTATE.

A MONKEY'S DATE?

NO, NOT MONKEYS, DEAR PRINCE. MONKS

YOU MEAN THOSE BALD GUYS?

PRECISELY, SIR. THIS PARK IS NEAR ENOUGH TO THE CITY, BUT FAR ENOUGH TO BE QUIET AND PEACEFUL. THE PERFECT SURROUNDING FOR MONKS TO TRAIN AND MEDITATE, DON'T YOU THINK?

WHY SHOULD I GIVE YOU ANYTHING?

I CAN'T STAND ROTTEN MERCHANTS LIKE YOU. ALL YOU THINK ABOUT IS HOW TO MAKE MORE MONEY!

YOU GO ON TV AND SAY, "ALL HUMANS ARE FAMILY! MAY THERE BE PEACE IN THE WORLD," BUT I KNOW YOU'RE JUST A PUBLICITY HOUND!

HEH...

79

80

FATHER
!

JETA! LOOK HOW YOU'VE GROWN! HAS IT REALLY BEEN JUST A YEAR?

WHY DID YOU COME HOME ALL OF A SUDDEN?

I DECIDED TO RESTORE FREEDOM TO THE SHAKYA.

IS THAT SO?

I DIDN'T THINK YOU'D EVER FORGIVE THEM.

I DIDN'T EITHER, UNTIL A GREAT MAN CAME TO SPEAK WITH ME. HIS WORDS CHANGED MY THINKING.

THERE'S NO ONE GREATER THAN YOU, FATHER.

HIS NAME IS BUDDHA. I ASKED HIM TO COME VISIT US HERE.

THAT'S JUST NOT RIGHT.

YOU NEVER LISTENED TO OTHER PEOPLE'S ADVICE BEFORE.

YOU SHOULD LISTEN TO WHAT HE HAS TO SAY. I'LL MAKE THE KING HEAR HIM AS WELL.

HA HA HA HA! THAT'S A JOKE, RIGHT ?!

I ORDERED YOU TO FORCE THE SHAKYA INTO SLAVERY AND KEEP CLOSE WATCH ON THEM.

YOU SHOULD HAVE BEEN HAPPY TO PUNISH THEM!

FATHER, I DID HAVE A GRUDGE AGAINST THE SHAKYAN PEOPLE.

BUT I FELT THAT THEY HAD SUFFERED ENOUGH. IT WAS TIME TO FORGIVE THEM.

SHUT UP

SHUT UP

SHUT UP!!!

THOSE DIRTY SHAKYA HAD THE NERVE TO TRICK ME INTO MARRYING A LOWLY SLAVE! YOU WERE OSTRACIZED BECAUSE YOU WERE THE SON OF A SLAVE!

YOU'RE STILL OBSESSED ABOUT THAT, FATHER?

ZWOOSH!

84

GO BACK AND KILL THE SHAKYA, MAKE THEM PAY FOR HAVING HUMILIATED A KING!

I WON'T ALLOW A DISLOYAL PRINCE TO BECOME MY SUCCESSOR.

...

DID YOU TALK WITH GRANDPA? HOW'D IT GO?

JETA...

WOULD YOU LIKE ME TO BECOME KING AS SOON AS POSSIBLE?

OF COURSE, FATHER.

I DON'T UNDERSTAND WHY YOU HAVEN'T BEEN MADE KING ALREADY.

ISN'T GRANDPA TOO OLD TO STILL BE RULING THE COUNTRY?

HE'S TOO PROUD.

87

OH? AND WHY IS THAT?

I HAVE SO MUCH MONEY PILED UP IT'S STARTING TO GROW MOLD. I HAVE VILLAS IN THE TROPICS. I HAVE SO MANY MISTRESSES THAT I'VE LOST COUNT. NOW I WANT TO DO SOMETHING FOR THE GREATER GOOD.

YOU ALREADY GIVE GENEROUSLY TO THE POOR, DON'T YOU?

YES, I DO. THERE ARE MANY CHARITIES THAT I DONATE TO. THAT'S NOT WHAT I MEAN.

I WANT TO BECOME...

A PATRON OF THE ARTS! I WANT TO GO DOWN IN HISTORY AS THE MOST GENEROUS SPONSOR OF ALL THINGS CULTURAL!

OH HO, NOW I SEE.

YOU JUST WANT TO HAVE YOUR NAME WRITTEN IN THE HISTORY BOOKS, RIGHT?

WELL, YES, OF COURSE. I WANT TO BE REMEMBERED KINDLY BY POSTERITY.

ANY IDEAS? WHAT DO YOU THINK I SHOULD DO THAT WOULD BE WORTHY OF A BRONZE STATUE MADE IN MY LIKENESS?

WHY NOT DONATE TO THE U.N. REFUGEE AGENCY?

SPONSOR THE NEXT WORLD FAIR!

BE QUIET!

AH! I HAVE AN IDEA!

THERE'S A CEMETERY A LITTLE WAYS FROM HERE CALLED SITAVANA. IT'S A NICE, QUIET PLACE THAT'S GOOD FOR THINKING. I GO THERE OFTEN JUST FOR A STROLL.

WHY DON'T YOU GO THERE TOMORROW MORNING?

SITAVANA, EH?

YOU'VE GOTTA BE KIDDING ME. WHO COULD EVER COME UP WITH A GOOD IDEA IN SUCH A DESOLATE PLACE?

92

DEAR SIR

YOU WORRY ABOUT YOUR ASSETS. YOU WORRY ABOUT YOUR FORTUNE. YOU WORRY ABOUT EVERYTHING, AND SO YOU FEAR DEATH.

THAT IS TRUE...

LET GO OF WORRY; YOU'LL FIND EASE. YOU'LL BE HAPPY UNTIL YOUR DYING DAY.

BUDDHA! I AM A WEALTHY MERCHANT FROM KOSALA. MY NAME IS SUDATTA. IF I MAY, I'D LIKE TO HEAR MORE OF WHAT YOU HAVE TO SAY. I WANT TO LEARN HOW TO HAVE A HAPPY LIFE!

I'LL VISIT KOSALA SOMEDAY. WE SHALL MEET AGAIN, TRAVELER.

SHOW THOSE NOBLES WHAT WE TOWNSFOLK ARE MADE OF!

JUST YOU WAIT!

MISTER SUDATTA! WE DON'T SEEM TO HAVE ENOUGH COINS!

...YES...

REMEMBER, I SAID TO COVER THE ENTIRE PARK WITH GOLD!

YES, MILORD...

WHAT ARE YOU WAITING FOR? YOU'RE NOT EVEN CLOSE TO FINISHING.

DON'T TELL ME YOU'VE USED UP ALL YOUR GOLD COINS ALREADY!

SO? ARE YOU BROKE? I THOUGHT YOU WERE A MILLIONAIRE.

NO, SIR! DON'T WORRY! I'VE GOT TONS OF MONEY LEFT!

THEN QUIT GRUMBLING AND GET BACK TO WORK!

IF YOU TAKE TOO LONG I MIGHT CHANGE MY MIND ABOUT SELLING!

103

SUDATTA, PLEASE STOP THIS FOOLISHNESS.

JUST GO AND APOLOGIZE TO THE PRINCE.

WHY SHOULD I APOLOGIZE TO HIM?!

THAT SPOILED HOODLUM OF A PRINCE DOESN'T KNOW THE FIRST THING ABOUT MONEY!

AND YET HE DARES TO LOOK DOWN HIS NOSE AT US! I WON'T BOW DOWN TO THE LIKES OF HIM!

I UNDERSTAND, SIR...

BUT YOU'RE BROKE...

YEAH, I KNOW...

I'VE GOTTA MAKE MORE MONEY.

I'VE GOT IT!

I'LL SELL THIS MANSION!

I'LL SELL ALL OF MY SLAVES!

I'LL FIRE EVERY LAST ONE OF MY ADVISORS!

THIS IS INSANITY!!

105

107

CITY OF SAVATTHI
THE SLUM DISTRICT

HEY HAVE Y'ALL SEEN THE NEW GUY?

YEAH, I'VE SEEN 'IM. USED TO BE RICH. USED TO GIVE TO US POOR FOLKS.

WHERE IS THAT MAN NOW?

IT'S THE PRINCE!

I CAN'T BELIEVE YER LORDSHIP'D COME TO THIS HERE FILTHY PLACE...

THE MAN LIVES IN THESE BEGGAR QUARTERS?

I DUNNO WHAT TO SAY...

Y-YESSIR! HE'S IN THE SMALLEST, DIRTIEST HUT, OVER THERE!

HEY THERE, RICH MAN!

OR RATHER, SUDATTA THE PENNILESS... HOW DO YOU FEEL? HUNGRY? PATHETIC?

NO SIR, QUITE THE OPPOSITE, DEAR PRINCE.

HEY, ARE YOU GIVING UP? IF YOU ADMIT DEFEAT I'LL GIVE YOU YOUR MONEY BACK!

NO, PLEASE LEAVE MY MONEY RIGHT WHERE IT IS. I'LL COVER THAT PARK WITH COINS, EVEN IF IT TAKES ME THE REST OF MY LIFE.

PLEASE WAIT 30 YEARS. THEN, THAT GARDEN...

UNTIL THAT DAY I'LL LIVE IN THIS HUT AND BEG.

ARE YOU JOKING? YOU'RE GONNA WASTE YOUR WHOLE LIFE LIKE THIS? WHAT'S THE POINT?

IT'S NOT A WASTE. I'M HAPPY. I DON'T THINK I'VE EVER BEEN THIS HAPPY BEFORE.

WHEN I WAS RICH, I WAS ALWAYS PARANOID ABOUT LOSING MY MONEY, OR SOMEONE STEALING MY TREASURES.

NOT A DAY WENT BY THAT I WASN'T WORRIED TO DEATH.

BUT NOW, I DON'T HAVE ANY MONEY, SO I DON'T HAVE A CARE IN THE WORLD. I'M HAPPY ALL THE TIME NOW.

CHAPTER ELEVEN

TRAPPED

PRINCE CRYSTAL!

THERE'S A GROUP OF MONKS SLEEPING IN THE FOREST JUST AHEAD.

JUDGING BY THEIR LOOKS, I'D SAY THEY'RE SHAKYA.

SHALL I ORDER THE MEN TO KILL THEM?

DON'T BOTHER ASKING STUPID QUESTIONS! OF COURSE, KILL THEM! DON'T LET A SINGLE SHAKYA SURVIVE!

118

FORGET ABOUT THAT. WHY ARE YOU DRESSED FOR BATTLE?

UHM... W-WELL...

ARE YOU GOING BACK TO KAPILAVASTU?

...YES...

ARE YOU GOING TO DESTROY THE SHAKYA?

THIS WASN'T YOUR IDEA, WAS IT.

NO...

IT'S JUST A SHOW OF POWER.

POWER? SO THIS IS YOUR WAY OF IMPRESSING YOUR FATHER?

NO! THAT'S NOT IT!

MY FATHER SAID THAT IF I DIDN'T KILL THE SHAKYA THEN I WASN'T WORTHY OF THE THRONE...

THE KING IS THE ONLY PARENT I HAVE.

MY FATHER HATES THE SHAKYA, SO HE ORDERED THEIR DESTRUCTION. I AM OBLIGED TO FOLLOW HIS ORDERS, NOT JUST BECAUSE HE'S THE KING, BUT BECAUSE HE'S MY FATHER.

DO YOU BELIEVE IN EVERYTHING YOUR FATHER SAYS? DO YOU REALLY FOLLOW EVERY COMMAND THAT HE GIVES?

NO...

I DON'T JUST BLINDLY FOLLOW HIM, BUT...

BUT IF I DON'T OBEY MY FATHER...

I'D SET A POOR EXAMPLE FOR MY CHILDREN. THEY WOULD GROW UP TO BE DISOBEDIENT, TOO.

I FEEL I MUST OBEY MY FATHER, FOR MY CHILDREN'S SAKE.

YOU'RE WRONG. IF YOU DON'T BELIEVE IN A COMMAND, WHETHER IT CAME FROM KING OR BRAHMIN, YOU NEED NOT OBEY.

WHAT?

121

THERE ARE SOME LEFTOVERS HERE. IF YOU'D LIKE, PLEASE TAKE THEM.

ONE MONK SAID THAT IT WOULD BE RUDE TO TURN HIS NOSE UP AT SOMETHING THAT I HAD OFFERED HIM.

SUPPERTIME !!

THE OTHER MONK SAID:

I APPRECIATE THE OFFER. HOWEVER I CAME HERE TO LISTEN TO YOU PREACH.

I WOULD NEVER THINK OF TAKING ANYTHING FROM YOU.

EVEN THOUGH HE LOOKED LIKE HE WOULD COLLAPSE FROM HUNGER, HE JUST WALKED AWAY.

SO, HERE IS MY QUESTION FOR YOU.

WHAT WOULD YOU HAVE DONE? WHICH MONK DO YOU THINK MADE THE CORRECT CHOICE?

IF I WAS THERE... I'D HAVE FELT OBLIGED TO TAKE THE FOOD. IT WOULD HAVE BEEN WASTED OTHER- WISE.

IF THAT'S TRUE, ANANDA, THEN YOU STILL DO NOT KNOW ME. AFTER ALL OUR TIME TOGETHER!

WHAT I HAVE BEEN TRYING TO TEACH YOU ALL IS HOW TO LIVE. FOR THAT PURPOSE I'VE JOURNEYED, AND WILL JOURNEY, ALL MY LIFE.

AND YOU WISH TO RECEIVE SOMETHING ELSE FROM ME? DO YOU FOLLOW ME BECAUSE YOU WANT TO BE FED?

NO, SIR!

WHEN A STUDENT GRADUATES, HE IS NO LONGER ABLE TO SEE HIS TEACHER EVERYDAY. BUT THE LESSONS HE LEARNED WILL REMAIN.

I WILL DIE SOMEDAY, BUT I WILL LEAVE MY TEACHINGS TO YOU. YOU'LL EACH HAVE TO LIVE ON YOUR OWN

RELYING ON YOUR OWN SELVES!

125

LET GO, I SAID !!

I WON'T LET A COWARD RULE THIS COUNTRY!

IF YOU'RE TOO LILY-LIVERED FOR THE JOB...

THEN I'LL CHOOSE A STRONGER, TOUGHER AND BRAVER MAN TO BE MY HEIR! THAT'S WHAT I'LL DO!

HM?

THAT'S FATHER'S FAVORITE WRESTLING CHAMP.

WAS HE SERIOUS...?

OOTANG, COME OVER HERE.

BLAAAAAH!

THERE'S NO ONE ANYWHERE NEAR AS STRONG AS YOU ARE IN THE COUNTRY. I'VE GOT BIG PLANS FOR YOU.

I THINK WELL OF YOU. SO MUCH SO THAT I'D LIKE TO ADOPT YOU AS MY SON, HOW'S THAT?

BUH GYA-AA!

IS DAT TWOO?

AHA... OK, STOP LICKING ME...

YA GONNA MAKE ME YA SONNY! GAH! ME SO HAPPEEE!

THESE ARE THE RESULTS FROM THE EXAMINATION.

SO YOU'RE SAYING THAT

THE KING IS TOO SICK TO RULE?

IT'LL TAKE A HUNDRED YEARS TO CURE HIM. WRITE THAT DOWN.

WE HAVE NO CHOICE BUT TO KEEP HIM IN SOLITARY CONFINEMENT UNDER STRICT SURVEILLANCE.

COURTIERS AND CITIZENS OF KOSALA AND SUNDRY OTHERS! LISTEN UP!

KING PRASENAJIT HAS FALLEN ILL! AS OF TODAY, I, VIRUDHAKA, AM THE HIGHEST AUTHORITY IN THE LAND!

FROM THIS DAY FORWARD, I SHALL RULE THE KINGDOM OF KOSALA!

AS MY FIRST OFFICIAL ORDER, I COMMAND YOU TO PREPARE A FEAST FOR BUDDHA AND HIS DISCIPLES!

132

BUDDHA? NEVER HEARD OF HIM...

IF THAT BUDDHA'S REALLY SOME HERETIC, A CERTAIN SOMEONE MIGHT NOT LIKE HIM BEING HERE.

YOU MEAN POKKARASATI? THE ZEALOT?

THAT'S RIGHT! I'D BE AFRAID TO PISS HIM OFF! HE'S THE MOST POWERFUL BRAHMIN IN ALL OF KOSALA!

POKKARASATI WOULD BEAT ANY HERETIC IN A MATCH OF WILLS, THAT'S FOR SURE!

HE'S GOT A LOT OF NERVE TO TRY AND SNEAK INTO KOSALA...

HE'S GONNA GET ON THE KING'S GOOD SIDE AND THEN DESTROY OUR SECT.

I WON'T LET HIM GET AWAY WITH IT!

MASTER, I CAN USE MY MAGIC TO STOP HIM IN HIS TRACKS BEFORE HE TRIES ANY TRICKERY.

134

SUNDARI... WOULD YOU OBEY ANY ORDER THAT YOUR MASTER GAVE YOU?

EVEN IF IT MEANT YOUR DEATH?

MASTER, I WOULD GLADLY SACRIFICE MYSELF FOR YOUR SAKE. AS YOUR DISCIPLE I HAVE NO FEAR OF DEATH.

WELL SAID!!

THEN YOU MUST DIE FOR ME! YOUR DEATH IS NECESSARY FOR THE FUTURE OF OUR SECT!

A HERETIC NAMED BUDDHA IS COMING. YOU WILL GO TO HIM, LURE HIM OUT WITH SUGARY, TEMPTING WORDS.

THEN, WHEN THE OPPORTUNITY COMES, I WILL SLAY YOU! RIGHT IN FRONT OF BUDDHA!

YOU WILL BE REMEMBERED FOREVER AS A NOBLE MARTYR WHO GAVE HER LIFE FOR MY SECT!

I LIVE TO SERVE YOU, MASTER...

IN RETURN FOR YOUR SACRIFICE, I SHALL LOVE YOU TONIGHT.

IT'S AN HONOR TO... SERVE YOU.

HUBBUB

HUBBUB HUBBUB

HUBBUB

HUBBUB HUBBUB HUBBUB

BUDDHA!

WELCOME TO KOSALA!

137

PRINCE... I WASN'T EXPECTING SUCH A GRAND RECEPTION!

BUT ARE YOU SURE THE KOSALAN PEOPLE ARE HAPPY TO WELCOME ME? I USED TO BE PRINCE, AFTER ALL, OF THEIR SHAKYA ENEMIES.

THAT'S NO PROBLEM!

IT'S PRINCE JETA!

JETA!

THERE IS ONE PERSON AT LEAST WHO WISHES TO WELCOME BUDDHA TO OUR COUNTRY.

I'D LIKE YOU TO MEET HIM.

OUR RESIDENT MILLIONAIRE, SUDATTA!

AH! I KNOW YOU! WE MET IN MAGADHA, IN SITAVANA!

139

OBSESSED SUDATTA AND HEADSTRONG JETA WORKED WELL TOGETHER, AND THE CONSTRUCTION OF A MAGNIFICENT MONASTERY PROCEEDED APACE.

EVEN THOUGH SUDATTA WAS THE OWNER OF THE LAND, HE SELFLESSLY NAMED THE MONASTERY JETAVANA, IN HONOR OF PRINCE JETA.

BUDDHA THEN MOVED INTO THE EXTRAVAGANT, MANSION-LIKE TEMPLE AND SPENT HIS DAYS PREACHING TO THE PEOPLE OF KOSALA.

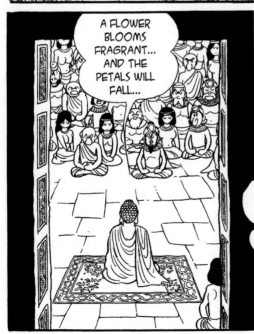

A FLOWER BLOOMS FRAGRANT... AND THE PETALS WILL FALL...

THAT'S BUDDHA. WHEN HE FINISHES HIS SERMON, LURE HIM OUT WITH EVERY SULTRY TRICK YOU KNOW.

141

ALL THAT IS WILL NOT STAND STILL FOR A MOMENT. ALWAYS MOVING, CHANGING... IT'S CALLED IMPERMANENCE...

THAT'S ALL FOR TODAY. THANK YOU!

I WONDER IF THE KOSALAN PEOPLE REALLY UNDERSTAND WHAT I'M SAYING.

THEY SEEMED VERY MOVED BY YOUR WORDS.

AH, I'M SO TIRED...I THINK I'LL LIE DOWN FOR A BIT.

THE WIND THAT BLOWS IN FROM THE FOREST IS QUITE CHILLY. SHALL I FIND A BLANKET FOR YOU?

NO, DON'T TROUBLE YOURSELF. YOU SHOULD GET SOME REST YOURSELF, ANANDA.

WHAT A DAY ...

142

143

144

145

146

147

148

DAY 1

DAY 2

DAY 3

DAY 4

150

I HAVE THE POLICE DOING A THOROUGH INVESTIGATION INTO THE MATTER AS WE SPEAK.

WE'LL FIND THE REAL KILLER IN NO TIME. I'LL HAVE THIS LIE EXPOSED AND YOUR HONOR RESTORED!

WAIT, PLEASE! THERE'S SOMETHING I'D LIKE TO ASK YOU.

?

I MET YOUR FATHER, THE FORMER KING PRASENAJIT, WHEN I WAS VERY YOUNG.

COULD YOU POSSIBLY TELL ME HOW HE'S FARING?

MY FATHER IS DEAD!

I'M VERY SORRY FOR YOUR LOSS...

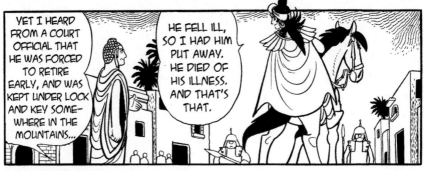

YET I HEARD FROM A COURT OFFICIAL THAT HE WAS FORCED TO RETIRE EARLY, AND WAS KEPT UNDER LOCK AND KEY SOMEWHERE IN THE MOUNTAINS...

HE FELL ILL, SO I HAD HIM PUT AWAY. HE DIED OF HIS ILLNESS. AND THAT'S THAT.

DON'T WORRY ABOUT SUCH THINGS, RATHER TAKE CARE OF YOURSELF.

OVER HERE SIR, YUP.

I HEAR HE'S LOCKED UP IN THERE, SIR, YUP, YUP.

154

IN HERE? NO WAY...

IT'S PITCH BLACK IN THERE. I CAN'T REALLY SEE, BUT I THINK SOMEONE'S THERE.

EXCUSE ME? ARE YOU PRASENAJIT?

HUH? W-WHO ARE YOU?

GET ME OUTTA THIS PLACE!!

LORD PRASENAJIT! MY, HOW YOU'VE CHANGED...

WHO ARE YOU? I DON'T RECOGNIZE YOU.

NOW I'M CALLED BUDDHA. I'M A MONK.

BUDDHA?!

ARE YOU SERIOUS? I—IS THAT TRUE? YOU'RE REALLY BUDDHA?

YOU TRICKED MY STUPID BRAT OF A SON! YOU'RE A PHONY! A DAMN HERETIC!

WHY ARE YOU HERE? DID YOU COME HERE TO SPIT ON ME?

NO, I HAVE NO INTENTION OF DOING ANY SUCH THING.

DID YOU COME HERE TO UNLOAD THE HATRED OF THE SHAKYA ON ME?

THEN WHY ARE YOU HERE? WAIT, LEMME GUESS. MY DAMN SON MUST'VE SENT YOU HERE TO TRY AND TRICK ME, TOO!

NO, SIR. HOW-EVER, THE KING TOLD ME...

THAT YOU WERE DEAD.

WHAT?

BUT I DIDN'T BELIEVE HIM, SO I ASKED A SERVANT ABOUT YOU. HE LED ME HERE.

D-DEAD?

 HE SAYS THAT I'M DEAD?

 SO I'M SUPPOSED TO BE DEAD ALREADY?

HE'S PLANNING ON MAKING THIS PRISON MY GRAVE?!

HE'S GONNA LEAVE ME HERE TO DIE A MISERABLE, LONELY DEATH?

 HE CAN'T REALLY BE SO CRUEL!

 PLEASE! PLEASE GET ME OUT OF HERE!

 I'VE GOTTA GET EVEN WITH THAT GOOD-FOR-NOTHING SON OF MINE! PLEASE, OPEN THE GATE!

WHY DON'T YOU TELL ME HOW YOU CAME TO BE LOCKED UP IN HERE IN THE FIRST PLACE?

158

SO YOU FOUND HIM AFTER ALL.

WHY DID YOU COME HERE?

I NEVER WANTED YOU TO SEE MY FATHER! NOW I SUPPOSE YOU'RE GOING TO ASK ME TO RELEASE HIM.

EXACTLY! RELEASE HIM THIS INSTANT!

I WILL NOT!!

YOU'RE NOT ASHAMED OF TREATING YOUR FATHER LIKE THIS?

LET ME REMIND YOU THEN!

FATHER TOLD ME THAT IF I FAILED TO KILL EVERY LAST SHAKYA, HE WOULDN'T ALLOW ME TO BECOME KING!

SINCE I DIDN'T, HE CHOSE HIS PET WRESTLING CHAMP AS HEIR TO THE THRONE!

...

KOSALA HAS NO USE FOR SUCH A KING! I THOUGHT IT WAS BETTER TO FORCE HIM INTO RETIRE-MENT BEFORE HE COULD DO ANY HARM.

BUT THIS ISN'T RETIREMENT, IT'S IMPRISONMENT! DON'T YOU THINK YOU'VE GONE A LITTLE TOO FAR?

I DON'T WANT TO HEAR YOUR CRITICISM ABOUT THIS, NOT THIS!

PLEASE LEAVE THIS MOUNTAIN AT ONCE! DON'T EVER COME NEAR MY FATHER AGAIN!

AND YOU, POPS...

KEEP UP THE JAIL-BREAK ANTICS AND I'LL HAVE YOU THROWN INTO THE UNDERGROUND DUNGEON! REMEMBER, YOU'RE PSYCHOTIC.

DID HE MEAN THIS THING HERE?

IT'S JUST A WEED!

...

THE ONLY LIGHT THAT EVER SHINES IN HERE COMES THROUGH THAT LITTLE WINDOW. IT ONLY LASTS ABOUT AN HOUR A DAY.

THAT TINY BIT OF SUNSHINE IS ENOUGH FOR THIS WEED TO GROW HERE, HUH?

BUT HOW IS THIS MY "ALLY"? I DON'T GET IT...

KAPILAVASTU

TATTA, I'VE BEEN SEARCHING FOR CLUES FOR DAYS NOW, BUT I CAN'T FIND OUT WHERE BUDDHA AND HIS PARTY HAVE GONE.

IT'S A SHAME, REALLY. YOU JUST BARELY MISSED HIM. IF ONLY YOU'D COME BACK FROM MAGADHA SOONER...

WHATEVER, IT'S FINE. DO YOU KNOW WHAT ALL THOSE LUMPS ARE?

THOSE ARE GRAVES. THE ONLY THINGS LEFT AFTER THE KOSALAN ARMY CAME AND SLAUGHTERED THE PEOPLE OF KAPILAVASTU.

THEY KILLED THAT MANY PEOPLE? DAMN THOSE KOSALANS!

WHY GET ANGRY? THE ARMY WAS SENT BACK TO KOSALA...

AND YOU'RE COOL WITH THAT?!

167

YOU'RE REALLY CHOMPIN' AT THE BIT, AREN'T YA?

I LIKE THAT.

NOT EVERY-BODY IN KAPI-LAVASTU

IS AN OLD HIPPIE FART WHO'S AFRAID OF KILLING OUR ENEMIES, YOU KNOW.

WHO'RE YOU?

THEY CALL ME BHARANDA THE KNIGHT. THERE ARE LOTS OF FOLKS WHO THIRST FOR REVENGE, JUST LIKE YOU.

IS THAT SO?

JUST LOOK AT ME.

THAT RAT BASTARD PRINCE ORDERED HIS TROOPS TO KILL MY WHOLE FAMILY. KOSALA IS MY SWORN ENEMY!

ALL OF US ARE ON YOUR SIDE.

EVERYONE HERE HATES KOSALA WITH EVERY FIBER OF THEIR BEING.

ALL OF US ARE READY TO STORM THE KOSALAN ARMY AT A MOMENT'S NOTICE.

THAT'S WHY I'VE BEEN DYING TO TALK TO YOU.

WE'RE READY TO HEAD OUT RIGHT AWAY. DO YOU WANT TO JOIN US IN BATTLE?

ARE YA KID-DING?

170

172

CHAPTER TWELVE

DESTRUCTION OF THE SHAKYA

177

181

184

185

186

188

AS THE BATTLE BETWEEN THE KOSALAN TROOPS AND THE REBELLIOUS SHAKYA RAGED ON, THOSE WHO WERE FED UP WITH FIGHTING FLED THE COUNTRY AND HEADED TO KOSALA.

SIR BHADDIYA, LOOK! THOSE PEOPLE ARE FROM OUR COUNTRY, AREN'T THEY?

190

191

KAPILA-VASTU IS NOW

THE GATHERING PLACE FOR HOT-HEADED ROGUES WHO'RE PLOTTING A WAR AGAINST KOSALA.

SHAKYA WHO WISHED FOR PEACE WERE TURNED INTO OUTCASTS AND CHASED OUT OF THE COUNTRY.

IT'S THE TRUTH, SIR. A KNIGHT NAMED BHARANDA IS THE INSTIGATOR. HE GOT A GROUP OF SHALLOW-MINDED, VENGEFUL MEN ALL RILED UP FOR BATTLE.

THEY REFUSED TO LISTEN TO ANYTHING WE HAD TO SAY.

SO YOU JUST RAN AWAY? AND YOU DARE CALL YOURSELVES ROYALTY? WHY DIDN'T YOU DO EVERYTHING IN YOUR POWER TO STOP THEM?!

GET BACK THERE AND STOP THE BATTLE, RIGHT NOW!

BUDDHA, PLEASE LET THE ELDERLY STAY, AT LEAST...

BUDDHA...

MOTHER! YOU SHOULD HAVE BEEN THE FIRST ONE TO STAND UP TO THOSE INSURGENTS! HAVE YOU TURNED COWARDLY WITH AGE?

OH....

192

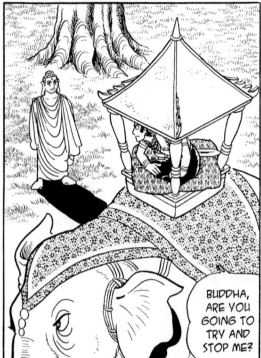

BUDDHA, ARE YOU GOING TO TRY AND STOP ME?

NO, I'M NOT GOING TO STOP YOU ANYMORE.

IT'S TOO LATE, ANYWAY.

I LISTENED TO YOU TWICE, AND TWICE I PULLED MY TROOPS OUT AND LEFT.

THIS IS THE THIRD TIME. I LET THE SHAKYA BE, AND THEY THANKED ME WITH AN INVASION. I HAVE NO CHOICE BUT TO DESTROY THEM!

I UNDERSTAND...

SUCH WAS THE FATE OF THE SHAKYA, THEN.

IF I SENT OUT MY FULL ARMY, WE COULD CRUSH A PLACE LIKE KAPILAVASTU WITHIN A DAY.

YOU'RE NOT GOING TO STOP ME? THEY'LL ALL BE KILLED.

...

MOVE OUT!

FATE...

THE SHAME OF IT !!

198

DAMMIT. IF I WASN'T HIT IN THE CHEST I COULDA TAKEN OUT 2 OR 3 OF THESE FAT SUCKERS...

DAMN UGLY SNOUT!!

OMPH!

TAKE THAT!

OOOH...

OH, MAN. I'M SO TIRED ALREADY...

YOU... I'VE SEEN YOU BEFORE...

BRING IT ON, YOU RAT BASTARD KOSALAN GENERAL!

201

202

204

WHERE'S THE CRYSTAL KING?! GET OFF YOUR ELEPHANT AND FIGHT!!

NOOO! BHARANDA'S BEEN KILLED!

...

IT'S OVER.

HOW FARES THE CITY?

208

FROM THE CAPITAL OF KOSALA TO KAPILAVASTU, BUDDHA WALKED

NOT EVEN NOTICING THAT HIS FEET WERE SCRAPED RAW.

AT DAWN, BUDDHA FINALLY REACHED KAPILA-VASTU

HE GAZED UPON HEAPS OF CORPSES IN A SEA OF BLOOD.

TATTA...

PART SEVEN

CHAPTER ONE

Sad News

WHEN NEWS OF THE FALL OF THE SHAKYA REACHED KOSALA, QUEEN YASHODARA, THE OLD KING SUDDHODANA, THE QUEEN MOTHER PAJAPATI AND THE REST OF THE SURVIVORS WEPT ALOUD FOR THEIR COUNTRYMEN.

BUT BUDDHA WAS THE MOST ANGUISHED AND GRIEF-STRICKEN OF THEM ALL. NOT ONLY HAD HIS PEOPLE BEEN EXTERMINATED, BUT IN THE END, IT SEEMED THAT NOT A SINGLE WORD OF HIS TEACHINGS HAD DONE ANY GOOD. NOT FOR THE SHAKYA, NOT FOR TATTA, HIS VERY FIRST FOLLOWER.

FOR 30 YEARS, I HAVE TAUGHT PEOPLE ABOUT THE LAWS OF HEAVEN AND NATURE. WHAT FOR? WHAT WAS THE PURPOSE? ALL MY EFFORTS PROVED FRUITLESS, IN THE END.

TATTA! EVEN YOU, MY FRIEND!... WHY DID YOU HAVE TO DIE?

216

217

NOW YOU SEE THE TRUTH ABOUT YOU PRECIOUS MASTER THAT YOU'VE SO FAITHFULLY FOLLOWED ALL THESE YEARS.

YOU'D DO BEST TO LEAVE HIM. YOU'RE TOO GOOD TO KEEP WASTING YOUR TIME WITH THAT PATHETIC EXCUSE FOR A MAN!

COME NOW, CUT YOUR TIES WITH HIM. YOU KNOW THAT I'M THE ONLY ONE THAT CAN MAKE YOU HAPPY.

I ALONE CAN MAKE YOU KING OF THE WORLD!

DON'T DALLY, ANANDA! COME AWAY WITH ME!

ANANDA, WHERE ARE YOU GOING?

BUDDHA.

ANANDA ...

BUDDHA, DON'T BEAT YOURSELF UP LIKE THIS. I PROMISE, YOUR EFFORTS HAVEN'T BEEN WASTED.

BUT LOOK WHAT HAPPENED TO TATTA...

I HAVE FAILED.

THAT'S NOT TRUE !!

WHAT ?

JUST LOOK AT ME.

I WAS REBORN THROUGH YOUR TEACHINGS! ME! A WICKED KILLER! YOUR SERMONS WERE THE ONLY THING THAT COULD CHANGE A MAN LIKE ME!

ANANDA !!

WHAT THE HELL ARE YOU SAYING?!

220

ANANDA, THANK YOU. YOUR KIND WORDS HAVE RENEWED MY STRENGTH. I FEEL BETTER NOW.

THE SHAKYA MAY HAVE BEEN WIPED OUT, BUT MANY REMAIN WHO BRAVELY RENOUNCED THEIR COUNTRY TO FOLLOW YOU. LORD SUDDHODANA AND LADY PAJAPATI ARE RESTING INSIDE.

PLEASE LET THEM BECOME YOUR DISCIPLES, BUDDHA!

HMM.

THERE'S ONE THING THAT STILL DOESN'T MAKE SENSE, THOUGH. WHY DID TATTA LEAVE VENUVANA AND COME SEARCHING FOR YOU?

I WONDER IF THERE'S TROUBLE BREWING IN VENUVANA.

I HAVE A FEELING SOMETHING'S UP.

RUMBLE

KRAK!

FATHER !

THAT VOICE... PRINCE CRYSTAL ?

YES, IT'S ME. IT'S BEEN A YEAR SINCE WE LAST MET.

YEAH, JUST ONE YEAR. BUT I FEEL LIKE I'VE AGED TEN YEARS

224

226

LEMME OUT! YOU ROTTEN SON OF A WHORE!

SLAVE BRAT!

WAAAAH! I DON'T WANNA GIVE UP THE THRONE!!

I DON'T CARE IF IT TAKES YEARS, IF IT TAKES DECADES... I'LL FIND A WAY OUT OF THIS HELL-HOLE.

KING BIMBISARA OF MAGADHA WOULD TAKE MY SIDE. I'LL GET OUT OF HERE AND GO ASK FOR HIS HELP.

AND THEN...

I'LL HAVE HIM SEND HIS ARMY HERE AND HAVE HIM CAPTURE PRINCE CRYSTAL.

UNTIL THEN...

I'VE GOTTA STAY ALIVE. I WILL SIT ON THE THRONE ONCE MORE...

229

I'M SURPRISED THAT YOU FOUND THIS PLACE. ARE YOU TIRED? WOULD YOU LIKE TO DINE WITH US?

NEVER MIND THAT. I'VE COME TO TELL YOU THAT THERE'S SERIOUS TROUBLE BREWING IN VENUVANA!

TROU-BLE?

DAYS AFTER YOU SET OUT ON YOUR JOURNEY, KING BIMBISARA

OF MAGADHA WAS IMPRISONED BY HIS OWN SON, PRINCE AJATASATTU!

HE WAS IMPRIS-ONED?!

YES. IT'S HARD TO BELIEVE, BUT RUMOR HAS IT THAT DEVADATTA SLOWLY POISONED THE KING. APPARENTLY DEVADATTA WAS MIXING POISON INTO HIS DRINK.

DEVADAT-TA?

NO, IT'S IMPOSSIBLE. DEVADAT-TA WOULD NEVER...

SO THEY TREATED THE KING AS IF HE'D GONE INSANE. PRINCE ORDERED HIM TO BE LOCKED INTO THE VERY SAME TOWER WHERE HE HAD BEEN IMPRISONED.

WHAT TREACHERY!

So then Ajatasattu ascended the throne. His first order was to name Devadatta as the leader of Veluvana. Devadatta himself showed us the official proclamation, but not everyone was pleased. The monks were divided.

I AM YOUR LEADER!

THOSE WHO FAVORED DEVADATTA'S LEADERSHIP FOLLOWED HIM TO ELEPHANT'S HEAD MOUNTAIN. BUT SARIPUTTA WENT THERE WHILE DEVADATTA WAS GONE AND CONVINCED EVERYONE TO RETURN.

DEVADATTA HAS KING AJATASATTU COMPLETELY UNDER HIS THUMB. HE EVEN GOT THE KING TO DONATE A LARGE SUM OF MONEY TO FURTHER HIS OWN INTERESTS.

THERE IS A GREAT DEAL OF AGITATION AMONG THE MONKS IN VENUVANA. THERE ARE MANY WHO WISH TO FOLLOW DEVADATTA. IT'S THE BEGINNING OF THE END OF VENUVANA.

JENTA, SOBITHA, UTTIYA, DARSAKA

PARIKA, RAKUNTAKA, PUTIGATTA AND OTHERS

HAVE ALL BECOME DEVADATTA'S DISCIPLES.

I CAN'T BELIEVE THIS.

DEVADATTA ENFORCES STRICT RULES. HE WANTS HIS FOLLOWERS TO LIVE THE BARREN LIVES OF ASCETIC SAMANNA. HIS WAY IS DIFFERENT THAN YOURS, AND THAT'S WHY HE'S ATTRACTING SO MANY FOLLOWERS.

HE'S DEAD-SET ON THE SYSTEMIZATION OF THE SECT. HE WANTS TO SET UP PARISHES. HE'S EVEN SET UP A MANAGERIAL STAFF WITH HIS CLOSEST ALLIES.

I HAVE MADE A GRAVE MISTAKE. I WAS FOOLISH ENOUGH TO LEAVE WHILE THERE WAS STILL UNREST WITHIN THE GROUP.

I'VE BEEN A FOOL ...

IT'S NOT TOO LATE!

PLEASE RETURN TO VENUVANA IMMEDIATELY. AND THEN

GO AND ASK TO SPEAK WITH KING AJATASATTU.

I WILL. DHEPA, GO BACK AHEAD OF ME.

TELL SARIPUTTA THAT OVER-COMING THIS INNER BATTLE WILL BE THE GREATEST ORDEAL OF OUR LIVES!

234

HI, GRAMPS!

OH! YOU'VE COME TO VISIT ME AGAIN!

I'M NOT ABLE TO COME AND TALK WITH YOU WHEN IT'S LIGHT OUT.

THANK YOU... THERE'S NO ONE ELSE ON EARTH WHO COMES TO VISIT ME, YOU KNOW.

REALLY? BUT YOU'VE BECOME SUCH A SWEET OLD MAN!

UHM... HE'S TALKING TO HIMSELF.

HE'S A NUTCASE. JUST LEAVE HIM ALONE.

A WHILE AGO, WHEN I WAS ALL UPSET ABOUT BEING LOCKED UP, A MAN NAMED BUDDHA CAME TO SEE ME. HE TOLD ME THAT I HAD AN ALLY HERE WITH ME.

AND THEN YOU FOUND ME, RIGHT, GRAMPS?

THAT'S RIGHT. YOU WERE JUST A SICKLY LITTLE WEED, BUT EVERY DAY I KEPT CLOSE WATCH OVER YOU.

YOU EASE MY HEART. I FEEL LIKE YOU COULD BE MY GRAND-DAUGHTER. IT'S NICE.

THAT'S RIGHT! AND THAT'S WHY I COME AND KEEP YOU COMPANY!

239

240

UNH!
O-OWCH
...

IT'S BEEN A LONG TIME SINCE I'VE WALKED. MY LEGS AREN'T WHAT THEY USED TO BE.

SCREW IT! I'LL MAKE IT TO MAGADHA AND ASK FOR BIMBISARA'S HELP IF IT'S THE LAST THING I DO!

SCALDING HOT SUNLIGHT AND POUNDING DOWNPOUR MERCILESSLY BEAT DOWN ON THE OLD MAN'S HUNCHED BACK. LIKE A STRAY DOG, BARELY KNOWING WHICH WAY TO GO, HE KEPT ON MOVING FORWARD.

PRASENAJIT KEPT PRESSING ONWARDS TOWARD HIS GOAL.

MAGADHA

HEY, BEGGAR! DON'T COME KNOCKIN' ON THE CASTLE GATES.

YOU WON'T GET ANY PITY FROM US. I DON'T CARE HOW TIRED Y'ARE!

WHAT ARE YOU MUMBLIN' ABOUT?

THERE'S NO KING BIMBI-SARA HERE! THE KING OF MAGADHA IS AJATASATTU!

WHAT?!

G-G-G-GO TELL K-KING BIMBISARA THAT...THAT KING PRASENAJIT IS HERE...

YOU'RE LYING!

R—REALLY? AJATASATTU?

COME BACK AGAIN YESTERDAY, YOU OLD FART!

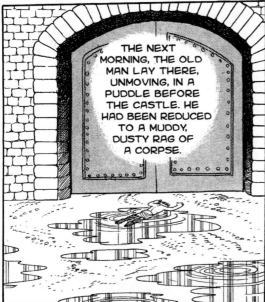

THE NEXT MORNING, THE OLD MAN LAY THERE, UNMOVING, IN A PUDDLE BEFORE THE CASTLE. HE HAD BEEN REDUCED TO A MUDDY, DUSTY RAG OF A CORPSE.

THE GATE-KEEPER HAULED THE CORPSE AWAY TO THE PUBLIC CEMETERY.

PRASENAJIT WAS NEVER ABLE TO SEE BUDDHA AGAIN BEFORE HE DIED.

CHAPTER TWO

DEVADATTA

FATHER WENT CRAZY. HE'S NO LONGER CAPABLE OF RULING THE COUNTRY.

SO WE HAD HIM GO INTO EARLY RETIREMENT. NOW I'M THE ONE IN CHARGE!

WHERE IS KING BIMBISARA?

IN THE NORTHERN TOWER. NO VISITORS ALLOWED. I HAVE EXPRESSLY FORBIDDEN ENTRY BY ANYONE OTHER THAN MYSELF!

BUT...

I DON'T CARE WHAT YOU'VE GOT TO SAY ABOUT IT!

BUDDHA, LISTEN WELL. I HEREBY FORBID YOU TO SET FOOT IN RAJGRIHA EVER AGAIN!!

MAY I ASK WHY?

DON'T ASK WHY!! WHY? BECAUSE I SAID SO! IF YOU DON'T OBEY MY ORDERS, I'LL HAVE YOU LOCKED UP TOO!

248

UNDER-
STOOD.

ANANDA,
LET'S
GO.

WAIT!
WHERE
ARE YOU
GOING
?

YOU'RE
THINKING
OF
GOING TO
VENUVANA
?

WELL, THINK
AGAIN. I GUESS
I SHOULD
UPDATE YOU
ABOUT
THE SITUATION
THERE.

YOU DON'T
REALLY THINK
YOU CAN JUST
WALTZ RIGHT
BACK INTO
VENUVANA,
DO YOU?

KING OR NO, THAT'S A TERRIBLE THING TO SAY! BUDDHA IS THE FOUNDER AND LEADER OF THE VENUVANA SECT!

LEADER, YOU SAY? OH, I'VE GOT A LEADER RIGHT HERE IN THIS CASTLE.

I'VE CHOSEN A MORE RESPECTABLE LEADER FOR THOSE MONKS.

NO WAY! THERE'S NO ONE BETTER THAN BUDDHA! I WON'T ACCEPT ANYONE ELSE!

I AM THE LEADER.

DEVADATTA! I WAS AFRAID IT WAS YOU!

YOU HAVEN'T GOT WHAT IT TAKES TO BE A TRUE LEADER!

ANANDA, DON'T GIVE IN TO ANGER. PLEASE CALM YOURSELF!

250

SO THE RUMORS WERE TRUE. DEVADATTA, WHY DID YOU DISOBEY ME? WHY DID YOU DO SUCH A THING?

DISOBEY YOU? HOW DARE YOU TALK LIKE THAT. THIS IS WHAT WE CALL PROGRESS!

BUDDHA, FACE IT. YOU'RE OLD. TO BE QUITE FRANK, I THINK YOU'RE GETTING SENILE.

THE SECT NEEDS NEW, YOUNG ENERGY. I WAS THINKING OF MAKING YOU CHAIRMAN OR SOMETHING, BUT YOU MIGHT AS WELL RETIRE, DON'T YOU THINK?

IF YOU LIKE, I COULD ASK THE KING TO GIVE YOU A PASS SO THAT YOU CAN COME AND GO FROM VENUVANA AS YOU PLEASE.

DEVADATTA HAS ONLY YOUR WELFARE IN MIND, BUDDHA.

THE KING MAY VERY WELL HAVE CHOSEN YOU AS THE LEADER. BUT NEITHER BRAHMAN NOR NATURE WOULD EVER CHOOSE THE LIKES OF YOU. YOU'RE NOT WORTHY OF SUCH A ROLE.

251

ONE OF THESE GOBLETS CONTAINS A POISON THAT CAN KILL A MAN ALMOST INSTANTLY. IF YOU TRULY ARE CHOSEN BY BRAHMAN...

YOU REALLY THINK THAT BUDDHA WOULD RISK HIS LIFE ON SUCH A DARE?

IF HE WANTS ME TO, I WILL ...

B-BUT BUDDHA! YOU DON'T HAVE TO STOOP TO HIS CHILDISH LEVEL!

THEN YOU SHOULD KNOW WHICH ONE IS SAFE TO DRINK. SO, WHICH ONE IS IT?

COME ON, BUDDHA.

I ORDERED BOTH OF THOSE CUPS TO BE POI- SONED. ONE SIP FROM EITHER ONE AND HE'S DONE FOR.

BUDDHA!!

...

NO, THIS CAN'T BE! HOW IS HE STILL STANDING?

DAMN! HE'S PROBABLY IMMUNE TO THAT POISON!

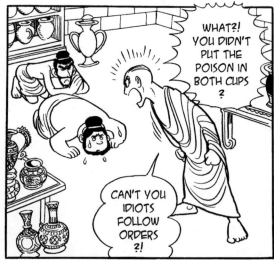

WHAT?! YOU DIDN'T PUT THE POISON IN BOTH CUPS?

CAN'T YOU IDIOTS FOLLOW ORDERS?!

WHAT? YOU'RE TELLING ME THAT BOTH OF THOSE GOBLETS HAD NOTHING BUT WATER IN THEM?

WHY DID YOU BASTARDS BETRAY ME?!

WE COULD NEVER POISON SOMEONE LIKE BUDDHA.

HE IS A GREAT MAN. HE'S LIKE A LIVING GOD...

LIVING GOD MY ASS!

I'LL HAVE THE KING FIRE YOU FOR YOUR TREACHERY!

I NEED TO COOK UP ANOTHER PLAN...

UNFORTUNATELY WE HAVE NO PROOF OF BUDDHA'S HOLINESS. THE RESULT OF THE TRIAL WAS A FLUKE.

WE'LL GO TO VENUVANA. WE'LL HAVE EVERYONE VOTE.

FINE.

LET'S GO TO VENUVANA, BUDDHA.

THAT'S A GOOD IDEA. THAT WAY EVERYONE WILL SEE BUDDHA AND REALIZE WHO THE TRUE LEADER IS.

255

IT SURE IS HOT. LET'S REST FOR A MINUTE.

BUDDHA, YOU SHOULD REST YOUR POOR, WEARY OLD BONES IN THE SHADE HERE.

I CAN'T FIGURE OUT WHAT DEVADATTA'S UP TO.

257

259

260

HELLO

 I'M ABOUT TO ENTER

 INTO

 YOUR MIND

 COME TO ME!

264

266

267

A NUMBER OF THINGS ...

NONE OF THEM WORTH WORRYING YOURSELF ABOUT.

BUDDHA, WHILE YOU WERE GONE SARIPUTTA AND MOGGALLANA WERE PUNISHED PRETTY SEVERELY BY THE KING.

THEY WERE TORTURED REPEATEDLY, BUT THEY ALWAYS REFUSED TO GIVE IN AND OBEY DEVADATTA.

THEY'VE BEEN WEAKENED SO MUCH THAT THEY STILL HAVE A HARD TIME MOVING ABOUT.

I DIDN'T KNOW... I'M SO SORRY.

DON'T WORRY ABOUT US. COME, YOU MUST BE TIRED.

DHEPA TOLD ME THE NEWS. I WAS PREPARED, BUT...

MIGAILA, DON'T GIVE UP. YOU'RE STILL ALIVE.

HOW DID TATTA DIE?

HE DIED LIKE A HUMAN.

BRAVE AND SINGLE-MINDED TATTA. IT MUST HAVE BEEN A HIGH POINT OF HIS LIFE.

LOOKS LIKE I'LL HAVE TO KILL BUDDHA WITH MY OWN TWO HANDS.

I'LL DO IT TO-NIGHT! HE'S EX-HAUSTED FROM HIS JOURNEY. HE'LL SLEEP LIKE THE DEAD. *HEH*

THIS POISON CAN SEEP INTO AN OPEN WOUND AND KILL A MAN IN 10 MINUTES.

I'LL SOAK MY NAILS IN THIS, AND THEN SNEAK UP TO BUDDHA...

AND KILL HIM WITH ONE LETHAL SCRATCH!

271

272

CHAPTER THREE

KING AJATASATTU'S SMILE

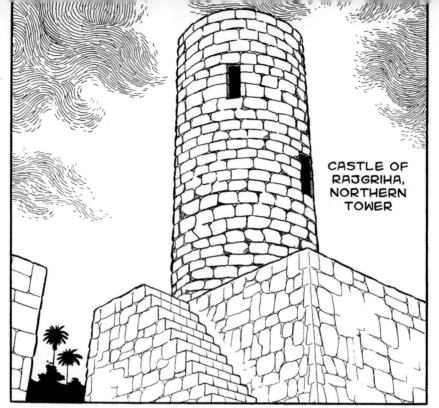

CASTLE OF RAJGRIHA, NORTHERN TOWER

GOOD DAY, GRAND DUCHESS!

I'D LIKE TO SEE MY HUSBAND. PLEASE LET ME PASS.

I'M AFRAID WE CAN'T ALLOW YOU TO ENTER, EVEN IF YOU ARE THE GRAND DUCHESS.

WE HAVE STRICT ORDERS FROM THE KING. WE CAN'T ALLOW ANYONE TO VISIT THE PRISONER.

THE OLD KING'S BEEN LOCKED UP IN THE TOWER FOR A YEAR. THEY NEVER BRING HIM ANYTHING DECENT TO EAT. AND HE ONLY GETS A LITTLE CUP OF WATER EVERY DAY...

KING AJATASATTU IS JUST WICKED. I KNOW THIS IS HIS REVENGE, BUT STILL...

HE MUST BE TRYING TO STARVE HIS OLD MAN TO DEATH!

THAT'S WHY THE DUCHESS COVERS HERSELF WITH HONEY AND COMES TO SEE HIM!

SHE LETS THE KING LICK HER BODY!

DON'T THINK DIRTY THOUGHTS WHILE READING THIS!

WHAT DID YOU SAY?!

ARE YOU SAYING THAT DEVADATTA IS DEAD ?!

HOW DID HE DIE?

HOW ?

HE BROKE A NAIL...

IDIOT! DON'T SCREW AROUND WITH ME!

THERE WAS POISON ON THE NAIL, YOUR MAJESTY...

WHY... WHY... WHY DID HE... HE WAS A GREAT MAN, A SAINT!

I LOVED HIM LIKE A BROTHER EVER SINCE I WAS LITTLE!

I'M GOING TO MY ROOM TO PRAY FOR HIM.

NO ONE IS ALLOWED TO DISTURB ME!

OH... DEVADATTA! WHY DID YOU HAVE TO DIE ?

281

YOUR MAJESTY...

ERM...

THAT LUMP!

I TOLD YOU NOT TO ENTER!

DOCTOR, WHAT IS THAT?

HMM...

PLEASE ALLOW ME TO EXAMINE YOU, SIR.

284

OWWW!

AAAHH! IT HURTS! HURTS!

WHAT'S THE MATTER?

HELP ME, PLEASE!

DRINK THIS, IT'LL HELP.

THIS WILL TEMPO-RARILY EASE THE PAIN.

WILL THAT STUFF MAKE DEVADATTA'S GHOST GO AWAY?

THAT TUMOR IS NOT BEING CAUSED BY AN ANGRY GHOST OR SPIRIT.

I HAD ANOTHER PATIENT A WHILE BACK WITH A SIMILAR KIND OF GROWTH. IT'S A BRAIN TUMOR.

HAH! QUIT TALKIN' LIKE A KNOW-IT-ALL, DOC!

I'VE BEEN PRACTICING MEDICINE FOR OVER 40 YEARS. PLEASE HAVE A LITTLE FAITH IN ME.

CAN YOU CURE ME? IF YOU CAN'T, THEN I'M GONNA HAVE YOU KILLED.

HALT!

MY NAME IS BUDDHA. I HAVE COME TO VISIT THE OLD KING, BIMBISARA.

NO ONE IS ALLOWED PAST THIS POINT!

BUT I'VE BEEN A GOOD FRIEND OF LORD BIMBISARA FOR OVER 20 YEARS.

I UNDERSTAND THAT, SIR. BUT I STILL CANNOT ALLOW YOU TO PASS!

PLEASE LEAVE!

I'VE HEARD THAT SENIYA HAS BEEN LOCKED AWAY THERE FOR A LONG TIME.

MAY I ASK WHAT HAPPENED?

IS IT TRUE THAT HE BARELY GETS ENOUGH FOOD TO FILL HIS STOMACH? IS HE BEING STARVED TO DEATH?

IT'S TRUE, BUDDHA. PLEASE COME JOIN ME ON MY VISIT.

HURRY! CALL THE DOCTOR, QUICKLY!

OH... OH... I–IS THAT YOU, D–DEAR..? I–I'M DONE FOR...

PLEASE HOLD ON! YOU'VE MADE IT SO FAR! DON'T GIVE UP NOW!

PLEASE, DON'T DIE! I BEG YOU!

L–LISTEN TO ME... I DON'T... DON'T HATE AJATASATTU. I GOT... WHAT I DESERVED...

OH... OH! Y–YOU'RE BUDDHA! BUDDHA... I'VE MISSED... YOU SO...

TH-THERE'S SOMETHING... I NEED T-TO ASK... YOU... BEFORE I D-DIE...

WHAT IS IT? I'M LISTENING.

PLEASE... T-TAKE AJATA-SATTU AS... YOUR DISCIPLE. HE'LL T-TAKE MY PLACE...

I WILL. I'LL GO AND SEE AJATASATTU ONCE AGAIN AND TRY TO MAKE PEACE WITH HIM.

I FEEL SORRY FOR HIM. I...WAS WRONG TO...AVOID HIM LIKE I DID... I MADE A TERRIBLE... MISTAKE...

P-PLEASE... I BEG YOU... SAVE MY BOY... AJATA-SATTU

AT YOUR SERVICE, LORD BUDDHA.

I'LL LEAD YOU TO THE KING'S CHAMBER.

AAAH! GYAAAH! OOOOOH!

BE STILL!

OH! BUDDHA!

291

I'LL TELL YOU WHAT I KNOW. WHILE DEVADATTA WAS STILL ALIVE, HE GAVE THE KING A SPECIAL POTION TO DRINK. THAT POTION...

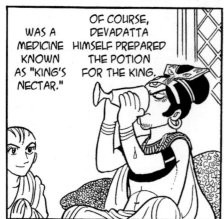

WAS A MEDICINE KNOWN AS "KING'S NECTAR." OF COURSE, DEVADATTA HIMSELF PREPARED THE POTION FOR THE KING.

IT WAS MEANT TO RESTORE HIS VITALITY AFTER SO MANY YEARS IN PRISON.

THE KING FELT SO GREAT AFTER TAKING IT THAT HE INSISTED ON DRINKING IT EVERYDAY.

BUT REALLY...

THAT MEDICINE WAS A POISON?

IT WASN'T POISON PER SE. JUST VERY POWERFUL. ONE HAS TO BE VERY CAREFUL WITH STRONG MEDICINE. ONE MISTAKE COULD BE DEADLY.

WHEN DEVADATTA DIED, THE KING'S POTION SUPPLY WAS ABRUPTLY CUT OFF. HE'S SUFFERING FROM WITHDRAWAL. LOOK, THE TUMOR'S GROWN OVER HIS EYES!

WE COULD TRY MIXING A BATCH OF THE SAME POTION FOR HIM TO DRINK, BUT I'VE NEVER WORKED WITH THAT MEDICINE BEFORE...

IS THERE ANYTHING ELSE WE CAN DO?

WELL, WE COULD TRY TO CUT OPEN AND DRAIN THE TUMOR, BUT THAT COULD PROVE DANGEROUS.

THERE ARE OTHER DRUGS TO REDUCE SWELLING, BUT HE MIGHT HAVE A BAD REACTION.

AHAN!

AH!

GHUH... UNH!

UNGG!

GUH... UNG...

OOHH... UNG!

GUH!

293

WHAT ARE YOU DOING?

I WANT TO TRY SOMETHING.

I THINK THE ONLY THING THIS MAN IS LACKING...

IS THE WARMTH OF A PERSON'S TOUCH!

HE DOESN'T NEED DRUGS OR KNIVES.

HAS NEVER FELT LOVED. HE SPENT HIS CHILDHOOD IN THE COLD RIGIDITY OF A COURT. HE'S BEEN SUBJECTED TO SKEPTICISM, MACHINATIONS, AND STRICT RULES HIS WHOLE LIFE.

MORE THAN ANYTHING, HE NEEDS TO KNOW WHAT SAFETY AND COMFORT FEEL LIKE.

SINCE HIS BIRTH, THIS MAN...

294

IF I CONTINUE THIS, MY WARMTH WILL EVENTUALLY COURSE THROUGH HIS ENTIRE BODY.

WITH JUST ONE FINGER?

I DON'T BELIEVE IT... THE KING JUST DROPPED OFF INTO A PEACEFUL SLEEP.

IT IS BELIEVED THAT THERE IS A FIELD OF ENERGY THAT SURROUNDS THE BODY. THIS ENERGY IS CALLED AN AURA. PEOPLE WITH VITALITY HAVE STRONG AURAS.
THE WARMTH THAT PASSED FROM BUDDHA TO AJATASATTU WAS PROBABLY ENERGY FROM HIS AURA.

HE'S SOUND ASLEEP. I'LL COME BACK TOMORROW. I'LL COME EVERY DAY IF I HAVE TO.

B-BUDDHA... WHAT HAPPENED? HOW FARES THE KING?

IT WAS AMAZING! BUDDHA EASED HIS PAIN JUST BY TOUCHING HIS HEAD WITH A FINGER!

HE MUST HAVE SUPERNATURAL POWERS. EITHER THAT OR HE'S THE WORLD'S GREATEST DOCTOR...

OH, I SAW A MOVIE ABOUT THAT!

I THINK IT WAS CALLED E.T., YES...

BUDDHA, ARE YOU E.T.?

DON'T BE SILLY. IF I MUST BE CALLED SOMETHING, I GUESS YOU COULD SAY I'M A DOCTOR WHO CURES PEOPLE'S SOULS.

BUT SERIOUSLY, I DON'T THINK THERE'S ANY PLACE ON EARTH LESS WELCOMING THAN THAT FRIGID THRONE ROOM.

HAVE THOSE GIGANTIC, FEARSOME STAIRS TAKEN DOWN AT ONCE!

DON'T ORDER ME AROUND!

BUDDHA CONTINUED TO TREAT AJATASATTU FOR *10* HOURS EVERY DAY. HE KEPT WORKING ON HIM FOR 3 YEARS. 3 WHOLE YEARS!

I TAKE MY LEAVE, KING.

I THINK THE SWELLING HAS COME DOWN A BIT.

BUDDHA, WHY NOT TAKE A DAY OFF AND GET SOME REST?

NGUH... UNH... HUH...

298

NO, I CAN'T TAKE A DAY OFF! IF I STOP TREATING HIM, THE TUMOR MIGHT GROW BACK.

IS THAT SO?

MINISTER

I'M HOPING THAT THROUGH THIS, I CAN SHOW THE KING HUMAN COMPASSION.

I GAVE MY WORD TO HIS FATHER THAT I WOULD HELP HIS SON!

THE TUMOR IS ALMOST COMPLETELY GONE!

BEAR WITH ME FOR JUST A WHILE LONGER.

SEE YOU TOMOR-ROW

BUU... BU...BU BUDDHA

THE KING JUST SMILED!

IT WORKED...!

SEEING THAT SMILE WAS LIKE...

SEEING A GOD SMILE.

GOD?!

...WAIT

I GET IT! YES! I FINALLY SEE IT!

THIS IS...!!

GOD, OH...!!

IT WAS A GREAT REVELATION.

BUDDHA WAS SO OVERJOYED THAT HE GAVE A SHOUT AND STARTED RUNNING.

HE RAN TO A NEARBY MOUNTAIN AND SHOUTED HIS JOYOUS INSIGHT TO THE HEAVENS

303

BUDDHA STOOD ATOP THAT MOUNTAIN, KNOWN AS EAGLE PEAK, AND VOWED TO TEACH WHAT HE HAD DISCOVERED.

YOUNG AND OLD, MEN, WOMEN, NOBLES, MONKS, MERCHANTS, PEASANTS... PEOPLE FROM ALL WALKS OF LIFE GATHERED AT THE FOOT OF EAGLE PEAK.

THE MOUNTAIN WAS DUBBED "EAGLE PEAK" BECAUSE THE JAGGED CLIFF RESEMBLED A GREAT BIRD LOOKING DIRECTLY UP TO HEAVEN.

PART OF THE ROCK FACE HAD BEEN WORN HOLLOW BY TIME.

BUDDHA TOOK A LIKING TO THE SHALLOW CAVE. IT WAS SHADY AND COOL.

HE HAD A STONE DAIS BUILT THERE, AND WOULD SOMETIMES MEDITATE. OTHER TIMES HE WOULD GIVE SERMONS. HIS NEW TEACHINGS WERE COMPLETELY DIFFERENT FROM THE ONES HIS DISCIPLES WERE USED TO.

HE DIDN'T TALK ABOUT THE STRICT LAWS OF MONKHOOD, OR GIVE STERN WARNINGS ABOUT LIFE. THIS RICH, SEASONED WISDOM MEANT FOR LAYPEOPLE HAD A WIDER APPEAL.

AND REMEMBER THAT THE TRIALS AND TRIBULATIONS OF LIFE ARE PART OF

THE EXPERIENCE OF SENTIENT BEINGS.

IF A PARENT OR BROTHER OF YOURS IS DYING OF HUNGER...

OR SUFFERS MISFORTUNE, WHAT NEXT? YOUR HOUSE MEETS RUIN AND YOU, TOO, WILL SOON SUFFER.

IT IS NARROW-MINDED TO WANT TO CURE YOUR OWN PAIN ONLY. YOU MUST THINK ABOUT YOUR FAMILY, ABOUT OTHERS.

IT DOES NOT MATTER WHO OR WHAT, HUMAN OR BEAST. HELP THE OTHER. IF IT SUFFERS, SAVE IT. IF IT IS IN TROUBLE, HELP IT.

WHY? BECAUSE ALL LIVING CREATURES ARE KIN IN THE HOUSE OF NATURE!

AT TIMES, YOU MIGHT SACRIFICE YOURSELF TO SAVE OTHERS.

311

LET ME TELL YOU A STORY...

AN OLD MAN

WHEE

WHOO

COLLAPSED IN THE MIDDLE OF A DESERT.

THUMP

HE WAS TOO HUNGRY, THIRSTY AND TIRED TO GO ON. THEN...

POOF

316

318

THE RABBIT SACRIFICED ITSELF TO SAVE THE STARVING OLD MAN, AND BECAME A GOD. THAT WAS JUST A PARABLE, ONE I HEARD A LONG TIME AGO, WHEN I WAS JUST A BOY.

BUT I'VE ALSO KNOWN A MAN WHO COMMITTED THIS DEED IN TRUTH. HE FED HIMSELF ALIVE TO A FAMILY OF STARVING WOLVES, AND SO DIED.

...

...

HE MUST HAVE SUFFERED TERRIBLY, AS HE WAS TORN APART.

OF COURSE, SUCH A FEAT IS NOT FOR ALL OF US...

MOVE

WHOA, LOOK! THE KING HAS COME!

BE SEATED, BE SEATED!

HIS MAJESTY HAS COME TO LISTEN TO BUDDHA'S SERMON!

RIGHT THIS WAY, MILORD. OVER HERE.

BUT EACH OF YOU CAN DO WHAT YOU CAN.

IF YOU ARE RICH, YOU CAN GIVE TO THOSE WHO SUFFER. IF YOU ARE STRONG, YOU CAN SUPPORT THOSE WHO SUFFER.

IF YOU ARE NEITHER RICH NOR STRONG, YOU CAN LISTEN TO THEM AND OFFER YOUR SYMPATHY, TELLING THEM YOU ARE SORRY.

THAT IS GOOD ENOUGH. JUST AS THE RABBIT IN THE PARABLE,

YOU WILL HAVE SUFFERED FOR ANOTHER.

LET US CALL THIS SPIRIT "MERCY"...

MERCY!

IT RESIDES IN EVERY HUMAN SOUL.

THAT IS WHY, WHEN YOU SHOW PITY TO SOMEONE WHO IS SUFFERING,

ANOTHER WILL SHOW YOU PITY WHEN YOUR DAY HAS COME TO SUFFER.

...I DON'T ...DON'T HATE AJATASATTU. I FEEL... SORRY FOR HIM...

FATHER...

IF YOU HELP SOMEONE, BELIEVE ME, ANOTHER WILL HELP YOU SOMEDAY...

CHAPTER FOUR

THE END OF THE JOURNEY

AFTER HIS NEWEST REVELATION, BUDDHA'S SENSE OF HIS OWN MORTALITY DEEPENED.

AN INCIDENT OCCURRED THAT MADE THIS FEELING DEFINITIVE.

BUDDHA!!

324

WHAT?!

BUDDHA, YOU SHOULD KNOW THAT
YOU HAVE ONLY 10 YEARS
AND 4 MONTHS LEFT OF YOUR LIFE.
PLEASE CHERISH THESE REMAINING YEARS
AND USE THEM WELL.
YOUR TEACHINGS WILL CONTINUE TO EASE
THE SUFFERING OF MANY SOULS
FOR CENTURIES.
FAREWELL.

YOUR FAITHFUL DISCIPLE,
MOGGALLANA

THAT NIGHT, BUDDHA SUFFERED A PAINFUL BOUT OF STOMACH CRAMPS. HE WRITHED ABOUT, IN DEEP SHOCK FROM THE LOSS OF HIS HEIRS. THE STRESS TOOK A SERIOUS TOLL ON BUDDHA, WHO HAD BEEN PRONE TO ILLNESS SINCE CHILDHOOD.

UHH... UNH! OOOO HHHH!

SIDDHARTHA! SIDDHARTHA!

WHO... WHO'S THERE? WHO'S CALLING MY NAME?

WHO ARE YOU...?

YOU'VE LIVED QUITE LONG ENOUGH, I SAY.

IS THAT YOU, MARA?

DIE!

YOU'RE DONE WITH THIS WORLD. DIE. PASS FROM THIS WORLD AND FIND ETERNAL PEACE.

I WON'T LISTEN TO YOUR WICKED ADVICE, MARA!

MY LIFE IS MINE TO LIVE!

BLECH!!

"COUGH" BLAAAH! BLECH... GEH...BLECH!!

THE REST OF MY LIFE...

DHEPA, I'VE BEEN THINKING ABOUT GOING ON ANOTHER JOURNEY.

WHAT ?!

IT'S BEEN A WHILE ...

BUT THAT'S FOOLISH!

HAVE YOU FORGOTTEN HOW OLD YOU ARE? AND DO I NEED TO REMIND YOU HOW WEAK YOU ARE FROM YOUR ILLNESS?

TAKING A TRIP NOW WOULD BE SUICIDE!

DHEPA, PLEASE. I DON'T HAVE MUCH LONGER TO LIVE ANYWAYS. I HAVE ONLY SEVERAL YEARS LEFT. MOGGALLANA TOLD ME EXACTLY HOW MANY.

SEVERAL YEARS?! AND THEN YOU'LL DIE? WHAT A TERRIBLE PROPHECY!

THAT'S WHY I'D LIKE TO SEE MORE OF VAJJI AND OTHER COUNTRIES.

I WANT TO CONTINUE TEACHING. THIS MIGHT BE THE LAST JOURNEY I EVER MAKE.

BUDDHA!

STAY WELL, MIGAILA!

COME BACK TO US!

BUDDHA SET OUT ON HIS JOURNEY WITH 500 OF HIS DISCIPLES.

THEY TRAVELED NORTH AND SOUTH, TO PATALIPUTRA, VESALI (VAISHALI), BHOGA, AND PAVA.

AND IN EACH LAND HE VISITED, BUDDHA TAUGHT THOUSANDS OF PEOPLE, RICH AND POOR ALIKE, THE PATH TO ENLIGHTENMENT.

STILL, BUDDHA HAD YET TO FIND

TRUE FULFILLMENT.

SOMETHING
IS MISSING.

WHAT ARE
LIVING
THINGS
?

WHAT
IS LIFE
?

WHY
DO WE
LIVE
?

WHY
DO WE
DIE
?

AS ONE GROWS OLD AND DIES, ANOTHER IS BORN, AND SO TAKES HIS PLACE. THIS SUCCESSION OF LIFE AND DEATH

IS NECESSARY. DEATH GUARANTEES THAT LIFE WILL CONTINUE. DEATH IS A NECESSARY PART OF LIFE...

ANANDA...I HAVE ONLY THREE MONTHS TO LIVE.

WHAT ?!

J-JUST THREE MONTHS? BUT...BUT THAT'S HARDLY ANY TIME AT ALL!

MOGGALLANA PREDICTED THE DAY OF MY DEATH. I DON'T THINK HE WAS MISTAKEN.

OH, BUT... BUT THAT'S...

IT'S NOTHING TO BE SAD ABOUT. EVERYONE MUST DIE. I'M NO DIFFERENT. DEATH IS INEVITABLE.

BUDDHA, WHAT HAPPENS TO PEOPLE WHEN THEY DIE?

YOU'RE STILL WORRIED ABOUT DEATH? EVEN THOUGH YOU'VE FOLLOWED ME FOR YEARS AND YEARS?

338

LOOK AT THIS.

A FEW DAYS AGO, THIS WAS A CATERPILLAR.

...

IN A FEW MORE DAYS, A BUTTERFLY WILL CRAWL OUT OF THIS COCOON AND FLY AWAY.

ALL LIFE IS LIKE THIS BUTTERFLY'S.

HUMANS THINK THEY LIVE FOR A LONG TIME.

BUT IN REALITY, OUR LIVES SPAN A VERY SHORT AMOUNT OF TIME.

THINK OF DEATH AS SIMPLY THE TIME WHEN OUR SOUL CRAWLS OUT OF OUR COCOON —OUR BODY— AND FLIES AWAY.

BUT... BUT WHAT HAPPENS TO THE SOUL AFTER IT FLIES AWAY?

DOES A PUPA KNOW WHAT WILL HAPPEN TO IT WHEN IT LEAVES ITS COCOON?

LIKEWISE, WE DO NOT KNOW WHAT LIFE WE WILL LEAD AFTER WE SHED OUR COCOONS AND DEPART.

BUT I'M SURE THE NEXT WORLD IS LESS RESTRICTING, MORE OPEN THAN THE WORLD WE KNOW WHILE WE'RE ALIVE.

SO THIS IS JUST A COCOON, EH?

THAT'S RIGHT. AND THAT'S WHY THERE'S NO REASON TO FEAR DEATH. IT'S JUST THE MOMENT IN WHICH WE PASS FROM THIS WORLD TO THE NEXT.

BUT THERE'S ONLY ONE BUDDHA IN THE WORLD! IF YOU DIE, THEN NO ONE WILL EVER HEAR YOUR SERMONS AGAIN!

DOGS AND CATS TEACH THEIR YOUNG, JUST LIKE PARENTS TEACH THEIR CHILDREN WHAT THEY LEARNED THROUGH EXPERI- ENCE.

I'VE PASSED ON MY KNOWLEDGE TO MANY DURING MY LIFE

AND YOU'LL TAKE WHAT YOU HAVE LEARNED AND PASS IT ON TO YOUNGER DISCIPLES.

THAT WAY MY TEACH- INGS WILL LIVE ON.

LET'S GO. I DON'T HAVE MUCH TIME LEFT.

341

343

WE DON'T GOT MUCH FOOD HERE, BUT PLEASE DO YER BEST TO FEEL AT HOME...

MISTER CHUNDA, YOU ARE VERY KIND TO SERVE US SO MUCH WHEN YOU HAVE SO LITTLE TO SPARE.

MM! THIS IS REALLY GOOD!

HAVE SOME OF THIS, BUDDHA.

MAY I ASK YOU WHAT THIS IS?

THAT'S A PATCH-GOURD, SIR, A SORT OF MUSHROOM...

THIS AREA IS FAMOUS FOR 'EM, SIR. BUT IF YER NOT TOO KEEN ON MANGA, Y'MIGHT NOT CARE FOR 'EM, SIR.

ACTUALLY, I FIND THEM TASTY.

IF Y'HEAD NORTH OF HERE, YA'LL COME ACROSS THE RIVER KAKUTTHA. BEYOND THAT IS KUSINAGARA.

THANK YOU SO MUCH FOR YOUR HOSPITALITY.

BUDDHA! WHAT'S THE MATTER?!

HE'S IN PAIN! QUICK, SOMEONE BRING A BLANKET!

OOO OH!!

HE HAS TERRIBLE DIARRHEA! I'LL TAKE CARE OF IT. PLEASE BRING ME A LOT OF WATER!

WE WILL.

I'LL SEE WHAT I CAN DO ABOUT GETTING MORE CLOTHS.

UNNH! UUUU HHHH...

ANANDA... PLEASE LET ME LIE ON MY SIDE... WITH MY HEART ELEVATED...

AHH.. THAT FEELS MUCH BETTER.

ANANDA... HOW IS BUDDHA DOING?

TO BE HONEST, I DON'T THINK HE'LL LAST MUCH LONGER.

SO YOU MEAN... HE'S DYING?

I WOULDN'T GO THAT FAR, BUT I DON'T THINK

HE HAS THE WILL TO GET OVER THIS ILLNESS.

THAT BAD?

SO... SO YOU MEAN WE'RE ABOUT TO LOSE OUR MASTER?

THAT MEANS WE WON'T HAVE TO DEAL WITH ANYBODY TELLING US WHAT TO DO! WE'LL HAVE NO MASTER!

WE'RE FREE! WE CAN DO WHATEVER WE WANT!

SHUT UP!

HOW DARE YOU TALK LIKE THAT ABOUT BUDDHA!

I WON'T EVER FORGIVE A WRETCH WHO WOULD DARE TO BETRAY BUDDHA AND HIS TEACHINGS!

I, ANURUDHA, WILL NEVER FORGIVE YOU!

SORRY ...

BUDDHA, TELL ME WHAT TO DO. I'LL DO EVERYTHING IN MY POWER TO HELP.

THANK YOU, ANANDA. YOU'VE ALREADY DONE SO MUCH. I AM IN YOUR DEBT.

THE SUN HAS SET. I'M FINE. GO AND GET SOME REST.

GOOD WORK, BUDDHA. YOU KEPT YOUR PROMISE TO ME. YOU CONTINUED TO TEACH THE WAY TO ENLIGHTEN-MENT UNTIL THE VERY END.

OH, HI, BRAHMAN. LONG TIME N—NO SEE...

YOU'VE MADE IT TO THE END. RELAX NOW.

I WAS AFRAID OF DEATH WHEN I WAS A CHILD. BUT NOW I KNOW THAT I SHOULD SIMPLY GIVE OVER TO NATURE.

SO YOU'RE NO LONGER AFRAID OF DYING, BUDDHA?

THIS SALA TREE WILL SOON BE COVERED IN BEAUTIFUL BLOSSOMS. WHEN THAT TIME COMES, YOU WILL LEAVE YOUR BODY...

AND COME AWAY WITH ME. I'LL SHOW YOU THE WAY. WE'LL GO TO THE HEART OF NATURE.

THANK YOU BRAHMAN. I LOOK FORWARD TO OUR JOURNEY TOGETHER.

HE KEEPS MUTTERING "BRAHMAN, BRAHMAN" IN HIS SLEEP...

SOMEONE'S HERE.

MUST BE A LOCAL MONK.

MY NAME IS SUBHADDA. I LIVE IN A NEARBY VILLAGE.

THE CHANCE TO MEET A GREAT MAN LIKE BUDDHA IS A ONCE-IN-A-LIFETIME OPPORTUNITY. PLEASE, PLEASE ALLOW ME TO SEE HIM.

WE CAN'T.

351

352

IS THERE SOMETHING YOU'D LIKE TO ASK?

Y—YES, SIR. I'M 90 YEARS OLD. I'M STILL CONFUSED. I HAVE SO MANY DOUBTS.

BUDDHA, PLEASE TEACH ME! GIVE ME A SERMON!

HEY! WE ONLY ALLOWED YOU A MOMENT!

DON'T PESTER HIM WITH QUESTIONS! BUDDHA'S VERY SICK!

ANAN—DA...

HELP ME SIT UP. I'LL GIVE HIM A SERMON...

BUT BUDDHA!

SUBHADDA, THERE ARE THREE THINGS IN THIS WORLD...

THAT YOU CAN PUT YOUR FAITH IN. YOU MUSTN'T DOUBT THEM.

YES?

BUDDHA DHARMA SANGHA

THOSE THREE

BUDDHA DHARMA SANGHA ?

BY "BUDDHA" I MEAN THE TEACHINGS OF HEAVEN, BY "DHARMA" THE TEACHINGS OF TRUTH. "SANGHA" IS THE GATHERING OF THE RIGHTE-OUS.

FOLLOW THESE THREE...

DO NOT DISOBEY THEM...

THEN YOU WILL AWAKEN.

TH-THANK YOU SO MUCH, BUDDHA!

SLUMP

BUDDHA!

354

THE SALA TREE IS IN BLOOM!

BUDDHA! PLEASE! HANG ON!

LOOKS LIKE MY TIME HAS COME...

I—IS THERE... ANYTHING THAT... A— ANYONE WANTS... TO ASK ME...?

ALL THAT LIVES MUST DIE. SUCH IS FATE...

BUDDHA! PLEASE DON'T GO!

AND SO
BUDDHA
PASSED AWAY.

THOSE DISCIPLES
WHO WERE BY
HIS SIDE STARTED TO WEEP.
SOME WRITHED IN GRIEF,
WHILE OTHERS
STRETCHED THEIR ARMS
TOWARDS HEAVEN,
LAMENTING HIS PASSING.

483 B.C...
THAT'S THE YEAR
GAUTAMA BUDDHA
IS SAID TO
HAVE DIED.

MORE THAN 2,000 YEARS LATER, BUDDHISM HAS SPREAD ACROSS THE WORLD, TOUCHING THE HEARTS OF PEOPLE IN CHINA, JAPAN, VARIOUS OTHER PARTS OF ASIA, AS WELL AS EUROPE AND AMERICA.

THAT'S BECAUSE IT TEACHES "HOW PEOPLE OUGHT TO LIVE": THE FOUNDATION OF LOVE FOR ONE'S FELLOWS.

BUDDHA WILL
ALWAYS BE FOLLOWING
THE OUTCOME OF THAT TEACHING,
FROM SOMEWHERE IN
NATURE'S GRAND BOSOM.

Osamu Tezuka (1928-89) is the godfather of Japanese manga comics. He originally intended to become a doctor and earned an M.D. before turning to what was then a medium for children. His many early masterpieces include the series known in the U.S. as *Astro Boy*. With his sweeping vision, deftly intertwined plots, feel for the workings of power, and indefatigable commitment to human dignity, Tezuka elevated manga to an art form. The later Tezuka, who authored *Buddha*, often had in mind the mature readership that manga gained in the sixties and that has only grown ever since. The Kurosawa of Japanese pop culture, Osamu Tezuka is a twentieth-century classic.

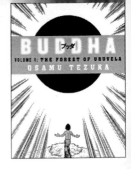

ENJOYED THIS BOOK? WHY NOT TRY OTHER BUDDHA TITLES BY OSAMU TEZUKA – AT 10% OFF! FREE POSTAGE AND PACKING IN THE UK.